MISTAKING THE COWBOY

A CONTEMPORARY CHRISTIAN ROMANCE

BLACKWATER RANCH
BOOK THREE

MANDI BLAKE

Mistaking the Cowboy
Blackwater Ranch Book 3
By Mandi Blake
All Rights Reserved

Copyright © 2020 Mandi Blake
All Rights Reserved

Published in the United States of America
Cover Designer: Amanda Walker PA & Design Services
Editor: Editing Done Write

Ebook ISBN: 978-1-953372-00-0
Paperback ISBN: 978-1-953372-04-8

CONTENTS

CHAPTER 1

HALEY

Haley Meadows had never been one to sit on the sidelines. An exciting life didn't exist without a few risks. That was how she'd ended up driving seven hours from Fort Collins, Colorado to northern Wyoming to meet a man she'd met online a month ago. She grinned as she imagined Micah's reaction when she showed up on a whim.

The drive hadn't been terrible. She'd sung every song on the radio at the top of her lungs until her voice hurt. Then, she'd silenced the music and created her own, tapping her fingers on the steering wheel to a beat only she could hear. She'd been an hour out of Casper when she'd stopped for gas and quickly jotted down the basics of the song.

Wyoming was an artist's dream. Even in winter, the silvery-white landscape begged to be memorialized on the pages of her sketchbook. No, her canvas pad. The scene might be vastly white, but there were too many variations for the lead of her pencil to capture. There were opportunities for color everywhere.

The pine-covered slopes of the Big Horn Mountains were barely visible in the distance, and the cottonwood trees were brown skeletons against the bright-blue sky. Maybe the Wyoming winter was more worthy of a song. She could inhale the cold wind and exhale a poem with minimal effort.

The upbeat tune of "Let it Snow" radiated from her phone in the cup holder, and she answered the call on speaker. "Hey."

"Are you there yet?" Her sister's voice was brimming with excitement with a hint of apprehension buried beneath the eager words.

"Almost. I can't wait to see him." Haley gripped the steering wheel and bounced in her seat.

Gabby sighed. "I hope you know what you're doing. Have I already told you it's a crazy idea to run off and meet someone you met online? I'm pretty sure Mom warned us about this growing up."

Haley was older than her sister by two years, but their age roles were often reversed. Gabby wasn't overly cautious. She was more moderate than anything. But compared to Haley's impulsive personality, Gabby was a straight edge.

"Speaking of Mom, you sound just like her," Haley said.

"Well, you sound like Dad, and that isn't always a good thing."

Pride bloomed in Haley's chest at the comparison to their dad. "Yes, it is."

Her mom was a gentle nurturer, but she'd found lasting love with Bill's adventurous heart. Despite their differences, they'd built a family together. A large one at that. Haley had three sisters and two brothers.

"You know I love you, but would it kill you to stop and think before you act for once?" Gabby pleaded.

"I did think. I thought about it a lot while I was packing."

"You're impossible," Gabby groaned. "I just hope this works out for you. Call me if you get any stranger danger vibes from this guy."

"So you can be here in seven hours to rescue me? Thanks for the offer, sis, but Micah is one of the good ones."

"You don't know him well enough to say that. Talking to a random man in sporadic messages for a month doesn't mean you know him. You've seen one grainy photo of a supposed cowboy, and you're already riding off into the sunset. Slow down."

"I'm driving the speed limit."

"No, I mean slow down your emotions. They're always running at full capacity, and you can't protect yourself like that." Gabby cared about everyone, even if her advice came across as demeaning.

"I'm not worried about getting my heart broken. I can take it. It's not like we're even really together yet. That's the point of this trip." Haley wanted a larger than life love story, and mediocrity wouldn't do. God only gave her one life, and she intended to love with her whole heart.

"You always bounce back. Just be careful."

Haley wasn't sure if her sister's words were meant to comfort or reprimand, but Gabby had stern feelings about Haley's flippant search for love. "Yes, ma'am."

She disconnected the call with Gabby as she turned by the rusty Blackwater Ranch sign. A solid layer of snow covered the ground, and she followed the tire tracks up a long drive.

Haley might be reaching a bit by driving out here to meet Micah without any notice, but she had to give it a chance. Gabby's words played in Haley's mind. She'd been trying to force relationships for years now, and while an epic love story would be fabulous, she was starting to think she'd have to settle for someone who would return her texts.

When Micah mentioned that he worked at a ranch, Haley had jumped online. The photos showcased beautiful rooms and stunning Wyoming landscapes, but the website layout was atrocious. She hadn't even been able to book a room from the sparse site.

After grabbing the phone number off the home page, she'd left a message. Five hours later, she'd spoken to a friendly woman named Anita who reserved her a room at the newly opened bed and breakfast. Anita cut a deal in exchange for redesigning the ranch website.

With an open reservation, she hadn't made any commitments on a checkout date. Truly, she'd been aching for a break from her messy roommate, Dana. Haley didn't want to kick her out, but she couldn't spend any more time cleaning up someone else's junk. She had work to do, and her customers depended on her.

A large wooden house came into view, and she leaned into the steering wheel. It was gorgeous, with snow on the roof and a wraparound porch dotted with rocking chairs. The structure seemed to settle into the land, becoming as much a part of it as the fluffy white snow.

Now, this was worthy of a painting. Places were easy to capture in visual formats like paintings and sketches.

She glanced at the photograph propped up beside her speedometer. Micah and his brother, Asher, stood smiling with one arm around each other. She studied the image of Micah once more, but she didn't need to. She knew the angles of his face by heart. As much as she loved still life and landscape art, people made the best subjects. Their emotions were fleeting, and if they weren't captured in the moment, they could be gone forever. Micah's big smile in the photo drew her attention most of all. It looked effortless, and she knew they would get along just fine.

A man stepped out onto the porch just as she was parking. She would know that face anywhere. She'd committed the dark hair and lean frame to memory weeks ago. Her heart raced just thinking about surprising him with a kiss. The brilliant idea had come to her on the drive this morning, and she'd been leaning harder on the accelerator ever since.

She threw the car into park and killed the engine. With a quick glance at herself in the rearview mirror, she hopped out of the car with an easy smile on her face. He was just as handsome in person as he was in the photo. No, he was heart-breakingly gorgeous, and nerves squirmed in her middle like snakes.

No turning back now. Just do it.

Her stomach flipped in anticipation as she closed the car door and took the first step toward him. "There you are!"

Snow crunched beneath her boots as she ran to him. Well, it was more of a jog, but she was fumbling the grace of each step and looked like a baby giraffe as she high-kneed to the porch.

The three steps leading to the rise of the porch were easier. She bounded up them and barreled into his strong chest. Thank goodness he was sturdy because she'd lost her own footing as he wrapped his strong arms around her.

She smiled up at him, lost for a moment in his amused grin, before remembering her intentions—the kiss.

Pushing up on her tiptoes, she smashed her lips to his and breathed in. Despite the freezing Wyoming air, heat filled her body from the inside out. She melted into his chest as he tightened his hold around her and returned her kiss. Boy, could this man kiss. It was everything her romantic heart had dreamed it would be. He kissed her as if he'd been missing her his whole life.

His fingertips pressed into her back, pulling her closer and deepening the connection. When he finally pulled away, he shook his head as if to clear a fog. "Wow. That's one way to say hello."

"Yeah." Her foggy brain couldn't manage a better response, but surely he got the idea.

"Who are you?"

Huh? Not the greeting she'd been expecting.

"What?" she asked.

His hands were still splayed over her back,

holding her close. "I don't think I caught your name. Am I on one of those hidden camera shows?"

The smile fell from her face, and she cocked her head in confusion. "Micah, it's me, Haley. I sent you photos."

His eyes opened wider, and she felt the swelling of his chest as he sucked air in through his nose. "I'm not Micah."

He released his hold on her, and she stepped back—more like fell back. The elation that had carried her here disappeared, replaced by confusion. "What? Are you his twin?"

"Nope." He stared at her as if she was a puzzle he couldn't figure out. His expression was void of the joyful surprise he'd worn seconds ago.

Haley jerked the photo from her back pocket. "This is you."

He took it from her and studied it before pointing. "This is me. That's Micah."

He pointed to the other man in the photo, and her nostrils flared as she tried to conceal her panic.

"What made you think I was Micah? How do you know him?"

Haley's tone was flat as she said, "He said he was the one in the red shirt." She couldn't tear her gaze from the photo. How had she gotten things so mixed up?

The man beside her huffed a laugh. "Micah is color blind. It gets him in a lot of trouble."

This time, she was the one in trouble. Shock took over, and she swallowed hard. It felt like razors sliding down her throat. "I've been talking to Micah online."

When silence threatened to choke her, she glanced up at the man she'd shared a passionate kiss with merely seconds ago. "You must be his brother, Asher."

Asher's eyes were wide as he nodded.

The implications of her actions settled around her, threatening to throw her reason for coming here into chaos. How had she kissed Micah's brother?

The door to the house opened, and they both jerked their attention toward the sound as if they'd been caught in the act.

A gray-haired woman wearing an apron stepped onto the porch. "There you are!"

Haley stood paralyzed next to Asher, unamused by the same greeting she'd used on the wrong cowboy moments ago.

The woman's sweet voice penetrated the silence that filled the space between Asher and herself. "You must be Haley. I'm Anita. We spoke on the phone."

At least one introduction was going well today, even if heat lingered in Haley's cheeks from her embarrassing mistake. "It's nice to meet you."

"I see you've met my son, Asher."

Oh, Haley had met him all right. She'd done quite a bit more than that. Pieces of the puzzle were clicking into place. If Anita was Asher's mother, that meant she was Micah's mother too. Maybe this introduction wasn't going so well after all.

Anita opened her arms for a hug, and Haley stepped into the embrace. "Welcome to Blackwater Ranch."

CHAPTER 2
ASHER

sher couldn't speak as he watched his mother wrap the auburn-haired stranger in a hug. They looked like friends.

What had he done?

He'd kissed Micah's girlfriend. He brushed the back of his hand over his mouth, wiping away the evidence.

Her name was Haley, but it might as well be Micah's Girlfriend. He'd do well to repeat that fact to himself every time he felt the urge to replay that kiss in his memories.

Haley pulled out of the hug with a fake smile straining her cheeks. The fraudulent expression was completely different from the lively, bold woman who had kissed him as if her life depended on it.

"Asher."

He jerked his attention to his mother.

"Haley is our first guest at Blackwater Ranch Bed and Breakfast. She's going to be working on a website for us while she's here." His mother turned to Haley, and the crow's feet at her temples grew deeper. "We're so glad you're here. You can call me Mama Harding, and if you need anything, just flag me down or get one of the boys to help you. I'll introduce you to my other sons at dinner."

Asher's mouth felt dry. Haley was staying here, and even now he didn't know how much longer he could hold his composure.

"Asher is the peacemaker in the family. He keeps his brothers in line, and he's always good for a laugh." His mother turned her adoring smile on him.

He certainly didn't think anything was funny right now. He wanted to crawl under a rock and stay there until Haley left.

He felt the nervousness radiating off her in waves. He had to get out of here, unable to look at the woman he'd just kissed without his blood turning to ice in the freezing air.

He tipped his hat at Haley. "It was nice meeting you. Please excuse me." He'd tried to keep his farewell neutral, but his formal tone only drew attention to his discomfort. He tucked his chin and stepped off the porch toward his truck. Getting far away from Haley was the first thing on his list. He couldn't think while standing so close to her.

He closed the creaky door of his truck, locking

himself into the safe space of the cab. Through the snow-speckled windshield, he watched his mother lead Haley into the house.

That kiss. He'd been shocked at first, but then everything had felt so right. When she'd stormed into him and greeted him with a kiss, he'd gotten lost in the moment. It had felt good to have a woman look so eager to see him.

But it hadn't been for him. Her excitement was for Micah. That happiness had nothing to do with Asher. The kiss and all of the emotion she'd put into it was intended for someone else.

He started the truck and punched the radio button. He needed to fill his mind with something besides Haley.

But he couldn't. Thoughts and worries filled his head, screaming louder than Conway Twitty crooning "Tight Fittin' Jeans."

Attraction—that's all it was. Haley was beautiful, sure, but he knew how to separate love from lust. He didn't know Haley any more than he knew which way the wind was blowing in Arkansas.

He parked in the loading area at Grady's Feed and Seed and went to find the old man. Asher could always count on Grady to lift his spirits. The white-haired owner never missed an opportunity to joke around.

After fifteen minutes with Grady, Asher's smile

came easier. He loaded up the bags of feed he'd ordered and settled back into his truck.

Except the heaviness was back. Was it guilt? He rubbed his hands over his face and straightened his hat.

On the road back to the ranch, he made a plan to talk to Micah. Asher would just be transparent. He'd kissed Haley. Well, she'd kissed him, and he'd kissed her back, but it was a mistake.

He definitely regretted kissing Haley. He would never have done it had he known who she was. Why hadn't he pushed her away?

Micah's truck was parked at the stables, and Asher headed over. His heart pounded in his throat as anxiety coursed through him. He'd never wronged any of his brothers before, and this time was only accidental. He doubted Micah would see it that way.

Inside the stables, Micah was saddling Sprite. Thankfully, no one else was in sight. Asher wanted to have this talk in private, in case everything went south.

Nervousness strangled him as he searched his mind for a way to start.

"Hey."

Micah barely looked over his broad shoulder at the greeting. "Hey."

"Um, so Haley is here."

"Who?" Micah stood to check the slack around the girth.

Asher ran a hand down Sprite's neck. "Haley. I didn't catch her last name. She said she's been talking to you online. Hasn't Mom texted you?"

Micah turned his attention to Asher with wide eyes. "She what? I mean, she's here? What for?"

Asher shrugged and raised his hands. "Don't shoot the messenger."

Micah rubbed the back of his neck. "I didn't know she was coming. I guess this is the part where you crack a joke about online dating?"

Normally, that's exactly what Asher would've done. Today, he couldn't find the humor in it. He tucked his hands into his pockets. "So, online dating? I never pegged you for a dot com romantic."

"How else am I supposed to meet someone? I hardly leave the ranch." Micah turned back to the horse.

It was true. How would any of them find a woman to spend the rest of their lives with, much less one willing to live on the ranch? Asher knew that problem like an old friend. The only difference was that his brother felt an urgency to find a wife, and he hadn't... until recently, anyway.

"She's nice," Micah said. "I think she said she was from somewhere in Colorado. I wonder what made her show up here."

Asher's chest ached, and he rubbed the surface to massage out the pain. He needed to tell Micah about the kiss, but short of blurting it out, there hadn't been a good time yet. "Mom said she's staying in one of the rooms in the main house and working on the website."

Micah's brow furrowed. "What's wrong with the website? I've been working on it for weeks."

"Apparently, she thinks Haley can do a better job."

"Oh, yeah. I guess she can. I remember her telling me she's a web designer now. It's probably a good thing she's here."

Neither of them spoke for a moment. This was Asher's cue. *Just blurt it out.*

Why wouldn't his mouth listen to his brain?

Micah slid his boot into the stirrup. "I wish she'd have told me she was coming. I'm leaving for Kansas City in the morning. That's at least a week-long trip if everything goes according to plan."

Asher sighed. "I forgot about the new bull. I'll go to Kansas City. You stay here."

Micah lifted himself up and swung a leg over Sprite. "No thanks. This is something I have to see for myself. I have a meeting with the vet next week to go over the disease records, and I need to study the herd's health."

"That's fair," Asher said.

Micah was the ranch manager, and a bad bull

could be the downfall of a ranch. It wasn't a decision to make lightly.

"I really don't have time to commit to someone right now. I don't know what I was thinking," Micah said.

"So, you're not interested in her?"

Micah shrugged. "I think she likes the idea of a cowboy more than she likes me. She asked a lot of questions about the ranch." He settled Sprite with a command and a click behind his tongue. "And the matchmaking site asks a bunch of questions about what you like when you start the profile. I made up a lot of it. I don't even have a favorite song."

Asher feigned outrage. "You're pulling my leg. Who doesn't have a favorite song?" Asher had at least ten favorites of his own. How could he and his brother share the same DNA?

Micah shook his head. "We'll talk later. Hunter needs help with a frozen feeder in the north pasture. I'll catch up with Haley at supper and set things straight."

Words needed to come out of Asher's mouth right now. Micah was leaving, and they hadn't talked about the kiss yet. Asher gritted his teeth, torn between spilling the secret and letting it continue to tear him up inside.

Sprite strode out of the stables, taking Micah farther away from the conversation that should've gone a lot differently.

Asher leaned his back against the wall and began banging the back of his head on the hard wood. The longer he went without telling Micah about the kiss, the harder it would be to share the truth.

Asher closed his eyes and prayed for guidance. He wasn't a fan of conflict, and that's why he was the peacemaker. It was starting to look like he could only solve problems if they weren't his own.

He'd pull his brother aside after supper and tell him what happened. It wasn't a big deal. It was just a kiss.

Even as he thought the dismissing words, he knew they weren't true. A kiss was never just a kiss.

CHAPTER 3
HALEY

"We're casual around here, but if your shoes or boots are dirty, leave them at the door."

Haley couldn't do much more than nod through Anita's introduction. What she'd seen of Blackwater Ranch so far was gorgeous, but she was having trouble focusing at the moment. Her embarrassing mix-up with Asher invaded her thoughts. She touched her lips where they tingled from the kiss.

They stepped inside where a few people were huddled in the far corner. Was that Santa and Mrs. Claus? Christmas was still three weeks away. Haley had officially seen everything.

"The menu for all meals is posted on this board here. You can ignore all the other notes. Ranching is a business."

Haley scanned the scraps of paper after Mama

Harding walked away—auction dates, hay for sale, and appointments for a horse chiropractor. Was that a real thing? The notices were well worn as if they'd passed over dozens of dirty hands.

Ranching wasn't a joke.

"Come say hello to our first guest!" Mama Harding raised her voice only loud enough to be heard over the chattering of the group.

Once Santa and the gang spotted Mama Harding and Haley, they quickly made their way over, laughing and playfully shoving each other the whole way.

"These are a few of our hard-working employees. Santa's alter ego is my son, Lucas."

He extended a hand to Haley with a slight bow. "Merry Christmas."

Haley relaxed and grinned. "Ho-Ho-Ho. It's nice to meet you."

Santa pulled Mrs. Claus into a one-arm hug. "This is my better half, Maddie."

Maddie grinned and offered a hand to shake.

A dark-haired woman with a megawatt smile wrapped Haley in a hug, breaking the hold she had on Maddie's hand. "I'm Camille, Noah's fiancée. He's around here somewhere. You'll meet him at supper." She released Haley as quickly as she'd wrapped her up. "I'll join you on the tour and let the Clauses play in their costumes."

Lucas tugged Maddie in closer to his side, and she giggled as he leaned down to whisper in her ear.

Camille rolled her eyes and waved a hand at the happy couple. "Ignore them. They're going to be Santa and Mrs. Claus in the Blackwater Christmas parade."

Haley perked up at the mention of Christmas. "That sounds fun. Are you going to be decorating for Christmas? I'd love to get some photos of that for the website."

Camille's eyes widened, and she bounced on the balls of her feet. "I'm putting them up this weekend! Want to help?"

"Count me in!" Haley's days at the ranch were filling up fast. She needed to reserve a few hours for work, but there would be plenty of time for that after the sun went down.

She followed Mama Harding and Camille through the main floor and up the stairs. The house was old and well lived in, but the construction was solid. Haley let her fingertips flow along the varnished wooden wall leading up the stairs. The house had character and history that piqued her curiosity.

"The boys have been working on these rooms for months. They've all been remodeled." Camille opened the door to a room and gestured for Haley to enter.

The fluffy bed took up most of the space, and a

dresser and chest of drawers sat in corners on opposite sides of the room. A window on the far side was
open, looking out at the vast reaches of the white
landscape.

"Whoa. This is cute!" Haley bit back the squeal
that bubbled in her throat.

Camille stepped into the room. "I thought so,
too."

Haley pulled her phone from the back pocket of
her jeans and made a note. "The website photos
didn't do these rooms justice. We'll definitely need
to update those."

"Of course," Mama Harding agreed. "Lucas took
those pictures with his phone."

Camille and Haley made the same cringe noise.

"You've got some work to do," Camille said.

Haley shrugged. "Hey, I can't hate it. I'm going
to love it here." She rested her hands on her hips.
"Do either of you know when I might get to see
Micah?"

Camille's brows shot up. "How do you know
Micah?"

"Well, we've sort of been chatting online. It's
how I found out about the place."

Camille gaped. "You're kidding! Oh, Lucas and
Asher are going to give you such a hard time."

Haley laughed. "Why? Micah seems nice." What
she knew about him anyway. Gabby hadn't been

wrong when she implied they hardly knew each other, but that was the point of this trip.

"Oh, Micah is *nice* all right. He's just not the romantic type. Online dating? I'm going to apologize in advance for the grilling you're going to get at supper."

"I already met Asher." As soon as Haley said the words, she wanted to cram them back into her mouth and swallow them.

Mama Harding hadn't said much, but she stepped up and put a hand on Camille's shoulder. "We'll let you get settled in. Do you need any help getting your bags from the car?"

"Oh no." Haley waved a hand in dismissal. "I need something to do. I'll make a few trips and get some exercise. I've been driving for seven hours, and my legs need stretching."

"Suit yourself," Camille said. "Let us know if you need anything. I'll give you my number, and you can text me any time."

Haley retrieved her phone again and saved Camille's name and number in her contacts. "Thanks. I already love it here."

Camille waved her farewell. "See you at supper."

Haley rolled the phone in her hand and let the last twenty minutes sink in. She'd come in with a bang, and now she had to figure out a way to patch things up with the two brothers.

She paced in the small room and opened her

phone to her favorites list. Who could she call that would understand, or at least help her figure out a way to dig out of the hole?

Not Gabby. She'd just say, "I told you so," and Haley would get an ear full about the kiss.

Beth was out of the question too. Haley's eldest sister would tell her to consider herself lucky to kiss a handsome cowboy and then dominate the rest of the conversation.

Her brothers were out of the question. They never had time to talk to her anymore, at least not without having to stop and scold a toddler every few minutes. Plus, her brothers preferred to remain ignorant concerning their sister's kisscapades.

Mom wouldn't understand either. She could always call her dad, but telling him she'd kissed a stranger would make for an awkward conversation.

That left Jess. Truly, the youngest Meadows sibling was the most likely to consider all feelings and consequences involved.

Haley pressed the button and reminded her lungs to breathe while the phone rang. She wasn't the type to ask for help, but with no ideas of her own, she needed someone to point her in the right direction.

"Hello." Jess turned twenty last January, but she still sounded like a peppy teenager.

"Hey. What are you up to?"

"Online shopping for a dress to wear to Christmas Eve dinner at Owen's house."

"Since when do you have to dress up for them?" Haley asked. "You're practically family." Jess and Owen had been together since they met their freshman year of high school and were inseparable.

"I know, but I think he might propose on Christmas Eve, and I want to wear something special."

Haley grabbed the foot railing of the bed to steady herself. "What? Really?"

"Well, I don't know for sure, but he said a few things this past week that made me think it was on his mind."

"I hope he does. He's a good man, and I know you'll be happy with him." Owen was as steady as they come, and Jess would gladly love him for the rest of her life.

Haley wanted a strong, steadfast love too, but she wouldn't last a week with a reserved man like Owen. She hadn't held down a relationship for more than a month, but that didn't mean she'd stop trying. She wanted a life of adventure with a man she could call her best friend, but she was beginning to believe that might be too much to ask for.

"So, how did it go? How is Micah?"

That was her cue, but the response clogged her throat. "He isn't what I thought he would be." In any number of ways, it was the truth. She had imagined the man she was talking to online to look like Asher in the photograph—young and grinning from ear to ear. She'd barely glanced at the other man in the photo until today.

"Oh, Haley. I'm sorry. Do you want me to meet you in Casper? We could spend the night there and hang out to get your mind off of things."

"No, no. Nothing like that. I actually haven't seen him yet. His mom said he would be around for supper."

"You met his mom before you met him? That's usually a step that comes later in a relationship."

"I think I've met most of the family already. I guess he's just out on the ranch or something. I wish you could see this place. It's beautiful here." Haley glanced at the snow outside.

"It sounds like you stepped into an episode of *The Andy Griffith Show*."

Haley looked out the window at the blanket of white covering everything in sight. "I don't think we're in Mayberry."

"You *are* going to be home for Christmas, right?" Jess asked.

"Do you know me at all? I wouldn't miss Christmas." The Meadows had always gone all-out for Christmas, and Haley got caught up in the holiday spirit easily. She loved everything about the holiday except the frivolous gifts. She liked being able to get by on a few essentials.

Christmas was about celebrating Christ. When had the focus shifted to tablets and gaming systems?

Micah was a Christian. They'd met on the Fated Mates site for Christian singles, but did he share her love of Christmas?

What about Asher? He looked like a man who could spread some holiday cheer. That smile of his would put her in a jolly mood in a hurry.

"Hello? Are you listening to me?" Jess asked.

"Sorry. I wasn't."

"Well, give it to me straight, why don't you?" Jess was trying her best to sound annoyed, but she didn't have it in her.

"I just have a lot on my mind." Micah. Christmas. Asher. That kiss.

Stop! Don't go there.

"I need to get unpacked and look at the Blackwater Ranch website again. I just wanted to hear your voice." She'd called with other intentions, but she was too chicken to bring up the kiss debacle now. She'd muddle her way through supper and sleep on it. Maybe she'd see Micah this evening and everything would be fine.

"I'm glad you made it safe. Love you."

"Love you too."

Haley tossed the phone onto the bed and groaned. She needed to keep her mind busy until she had to confront Micah and Asher in a few hours.

CHAPTER 4
HALEY

After hauling her luggage in from the car, Haley unpacked and pulled her laptop from her bag. She looked around the room and pursed her lips. No desk. It looked as if she'd be working on the bed.

First, she ordered a cheap lap desk and selected expedited shipping. She didn't want to work in the communal meeting room every night, as Mama Harding had called the big, open room downstairs.

Being able to see out the window of her bedroom was going to cause a problem. The scenery was too enticing. Despite the frosty air, the beautiful picture called to her.

Grabbing her camera, she snapped a few photos of the winter wonderland outside before testing out some angles of the guest room. The presentation was perfect for the casual, friendly atmosphere of the ranch.

Once the photos were uploaded to her laptop, she checked the ranch's website again and made a plan to focus on things she'd need before revamping. She'd need access to the other guest rooms for photos, and maybe Micah could show her around the ranch. She left room in her notes for things she might see tomorrow and want to feature on the site.

The sun was setting over the ranch, turning the sky oranges and purples she tried to commit to memory. It was a scene she wanted to paint later.

Checking her watch, she realized it was almost suppertime. She hung her camera over her neck and went downstairs to wait for Micah. If he arrived early, she'd get to greet him in private. She wouldn't be implementing her disastrous kiss greeting a second time. Lesson learned there.

Now that she'd used her fun, exciting greeting on Asher, she was nervous about meeting Micah in person. Embarrassment had replaced her confidence, and she wondered if Asher had already told Micah about the kiss. Should she tell him if Asher hadn't?

Mama Harding set a tray of crackers on the long counter. A lean, middle-aged man stepped up behind her with a handful of spoons and ladles.

"Something smells good," Haley said.

Mama Harding smiled as she arranged the bowls

and pots on the counter. "Soup is on the menu tonight."

"Perfect for the cold weather," Haley said.

The man stepped up to Mama Harding's side and extended his hand to Haley. "I'm Silas Harding. Welcome to the ranch."

"I'm glad to be here." Haley took his hand. "You have a beautiful place."

Silas wrapped his arm around Mama Harding's waist and pulled her in. The laugh lines around his mouth deepened as he smiled at his wife. "We certainly think so."

Haley lifted her camera. "Can I snap some photos of the meeting room? I want to get some during supper, too, so people will get a sense of what meals are like here."

"Sure." Mama Harding waved her hand in the air. "Do whatever you want. Make yourself at home."

Truly, Haley had felt comfortable here from the moment she arrived, barring the embarrassing mix up with Asher. Everyone she'd met treated her like a friend instead of a guest. She needed to find a way to capture that hospitality in the photos.

Two men entered through the door on the far side of the room. They hung their hats and coats on the rack, and one of them gestured with his hands, demonstrating a part of the story he was telling. They didn't notice her at first, and she lifted her camera to snap a candid photo. Their pants were smudged with dirt, and their smiles were wide and animated as they talked.

Mama Harding gestured to the men as they approached. "Haley, this is Aaron and Jameson. Aaron is one of my boys, and Jameson helps out sometimes."

Both men turned their attention to Haley, and their smiles remained in place.

The taller man with a dark beard extended his hand to her. "Jameson Ford. Nice to meet you."

She took his hand with a smile. "Haley Meadows."

The other man offered her a hand and leaned forward slightly. "I'm Aaron Harding. You must be the bed and breakfast guest Mama has talked about non-stop."

"You know it!" Haley shook his hand, noting the grease stains on it.

Mama Harding laid a hand on her son's shoulder. "Wash up. I made the chili you like."

"With the elk?" Aaron asked.

Jameson grimaced. "Don't tell Camille."

Haley laughed. "Camille doesn't like elk chili?"

Mama Harding pushed the men toward the washroom. "She was in a wreck last year. She hit a deer and had some lasting injuries."

Haley's hand rose to her chest. "That's terrible. She seemed okay when I met her earlier."

"Oh, she is now." Mama Harding waved a dismissing hand. "Anything that looks like a deer reminds her of the accident."

"I'm glad she's all right."

As if the mention of her name had summoned her, Camille entered the room and removed her coat and scarf. "Lucas, Maddie, and Hunter are helping out the Lawrences. They said not to wait for them."

Noah entered next, and Camille ran back to the door to greet him.

Haley's stomach rolled as her nervousness grew. Micah still hadn't shown up. She trailed a fingernail on the edge of her camera strap as she tried not to stare at the door.

Camille was telling Mama Harding about the recent work on a house she and Noah were having built on the ranch, and Haley got sucked into the conversation. Camille was a detailed storyteller, and Haley could almost picture the farmhouse with a green tin roof and a wraparound porch. She was so caught up in the conversation that she didn't notice anyone else had shown up for supper until a young boy raced into Mama Harding's arms.

Haley turned her attention to the door and saw Asher striding toward them. His smile was friendly, but it wasn't as genuine as the one she'd first met—before she'd mistaken him for his brother.

The little boy placed his dirty hands on both

sides of Mama Harding's face. "Guess what Uncle Asher let me do!"

Camille gently placed her hands on the boy's wrists and removed them from Mama Harding's face. "I don't think we want to know until you wash those filthy hands."

Mama Harding sat the boy down, and he barreled off toward the line for the washroom where Asher stood talking to the other men. "Hey! Uncle Asher let me break up the troughs today!"

"That's Levi," Camille explained. "He's Aaron's boy."

"He's adorable. How old is he?" Haley asked.

Mama Harding sighed. "He just turned four. He's growing up so fast."

Camille rubbed Mama Harding's shoulder. "Don't look so sad about it. You have four other boys who might give you grandkids. You're just getting started."

Haley watched the herd of cowboys laughing and joking by the washroom, and the strength of the family bond struck her in the heart. The Hardings had something special. The camaraderie was so much like her own family. She loved having lots of siblings, and the constant energy of the ranch made it feel like home.

She raised her camera to capture a photo of the men laughing when Asher turned to her. His smile was real and bright. When his gaze landed on her,

her breath halted in her chest, and she snapped the photo.

Lowering the camera, she watched as Asher's laughing smile turned to a closed-lip grin. He was still looking at her, and she couldn't tear her attention from him. His happiness was captivating, and she was drawn to it like a moth to the flame.

Mama Harding lifted her hand and announced, "That's everyone. Line up. Guests first."

Haley scanned the room for Micah—the other man in the photograph that she'd initially dismissed. He was making his way toward her, but his expression was blank, maybe even a little gruff.

Nervousness bubbled in her gut like a rolling volcano as she waited to meet the man she'd come here to see.

CHAPTER 5

HALEY

"Haley?"

Micah was tall, like Asher, Lucas, and Silas, but his facial features were softer and rounder, like Mama Harding's.

"Hey. Here I am." She lifted her arms instinctually, but when Micah stuck his hand out between them, she ungracefully transitioned into a shrug before grabbing his hand. She was a hugger, but Micah had definitely forced her into a handshake. This was already turning out to be a terrible meeting.

"I can't believe it," Micah said with little emotion.

Haley kicked the heel of her boot against the toe of the other one. "I wanted to surprise you. I looked up the ranch online when you told me about it and saw the bed and breakfast option. It sounded cool, so I got a room."

Micah brushed a hand over his tousled hair. "Well, welcome to the ranch. I hope you enjoy your stay."

Every word he spoke was strained, and Haley wanted to crawl back into her little car and drive back to Colorado like nothing had happened.

Micah gestured to the food counter. "They're waiting for you. I need to wash up."

She turned to see the whole family grouped at the beginning of the serving line, waiting for her to take the lead.

"Oh! Sorry." She laughed and took her place at the head of the line. "Everything looks so good. I can't choose just one."

Mama Harding pointed toward the closest one —a white, creamy soup. "Try the white bean chicken chili. If you don't like it, you can come back and get something different."

Haley narrowed her eyes at the gray-haired woman. "Do you cook all the meals?"

"I do. It's a full-time job feeding these men."

Haley picked up the ladle. "Then I assume anything you cook is delicious."

A sweet chuckle bubbled up in Mama Harding's throat. "Just sit wherever you'd like. There's a table to the side if you want some privacy, or you can eat at the long table. The boys usually eat first and talk business after, so make yourself at home."

Haley took a seat at the long, picnic-style table and waited for everyone else to sit. Silas was the last one through the line, and he stayed standing when he set his food on the table.

"Let's return thanks."

Every head at the table bowed, and Haley did the same.

"Dear Lord, we come to You today to thank You for the plenty You've provided for us and for sending Haley to our table. Please continue to guide us in everything we do. In Jesus' name we pray. Amen."

Haley lifted her head and swallowed the lump in her throat. The head of this family was praying for her by name as if her mere presence was a gift from the Lord. Silas sat in front of his soup and began eating as if he hadn't just called her out and claimed her—heart and soul—as a blessing to the family.

Everyone else began eating, and the room was quiet save for the tings of metal spoons clanking against ceramic bowls. Haley blew the steam from her first bite of the chili before testing it with her tongue. That first creamy bite flooded her senses, and she hummed in praise.

Camille lifted a spoonful of the same soup. "It's good, isn't it?"

"Delicious," Haley agreed. "I hope this is on the menu again before Christmas."

Mama Harding nodded. "I can make that happen."

"So, what are your plans for this vacation?" Camille asked.

Haley shrugged. "I don't really have a plan. I'm working on the website, but that won't take me too long. I'd like to see more of the ranch and get some pictures."

Noah lifted a spoonful of soup to his mouth and asked, "How long are you planning to stay?"

Haley grinned. "I figure I'll probably stay until right before Christmas."

Micah turned to her. "You mean, you're just staying until whenever?"

"Pretty much."

Micah's eyes grew wide, and he turned back to his bowl of chili. Maybe he was a planner. Haley didn't consider any getaway with an itinerary a true vacation.

"Where do you live?" Levi asked. His slender lips and the oval shape of his face resembled his grand-father's beside him.

"I'm from Fort Collins, Colorado."

Levi's eyes grew wide. "I know Colorado! Granny showed me on the map. And Alaska, and Florida, and Texas."

Asher lowered his brows at Levi. "You're too smart for your own good."

Levi sat up straighter. "Granny said I'm smarter than anyone else in our family."

Noah shrugged. "She's probably right."

Levi leaned over the table toward Haley. "I can teach you how to bale hay."

"We don't bale hay in the winter," Aaron reminded his son.

"I know, but I can show her how to do it."

Haley chuckled. "I'm sure you can. Do you help your dad and uncles out on the ranch?"

"Sometimes. When it snows or rains, Granny likes for me to stay in the kitchen with her. I help."

"Did she teach you how to make this chili?" Haley asked.

Levi shrugged. "I seen her make it before."

Haley eyed the matriarch sitting a few seats down from Levi. "You think she'll teach me how to make it?"

"Oh yeah," Levi said, nodding his head emphatically. "Granny is a good teacher. She taught me all the ABCs and my numbers. I can spell my name! L-E-V-I. It's only four letters, so it's easy."

While Levi talked, everyone else cleaned their bowls, and a few of the men went back for seconds. Haley had just finished her chili and rested her arms on the table when Mama Harding spoke up.

"Micah, why don't you tell us how you came to know Haley?"

Haley turned to Micah beside her. She'd tried to strike up a conversation a few times, but each topic had been overtaken by Levi. She couldn't complain. The little boy was a nice buffer for an awkward situation.

Micah scooted his bowl a few inches and began rapping his knuckles on the table. "We talked a little bit online."

Well, he certainly wasn't embellishing. She was getting the feeling that Micah was put out with her surprise visit.

Camille huffed and hung her head dramatically before snapping back up, her dark hair whipping around her. "It's like pulling water from a rock. Please elaborate."

Micah's face was turning red, so Haley stepped in. "We met on the Fated Mates site for singles and hit it off." She, on the other hand, had often been accused of embellishing. She liked to think of it as keeping an optimistic attitude.

Aaron laughed. "What? Micah is on a dating site?"

Camille shot Aaron a menacing look. "It seems he is, and it brought Haley to us, so shut it."

Aaron lifted his hands in surrender.

Noah barely looked up from his second helping of chili. "Be glad Lucas isn't here. He'd have a field day."

"Speaking of field days, what do you want to do while you're here?" Camille asked. "Blackwater isn't a dude ranch, but I'm sure we could find some fun to get into."

Haley tapped her finger against her cheek. "I don't know. I read on the website there's a creek here and horses. I don't know if I could ride, but I'd like to see them if I can."

Camille clapped her hands together. "Lucas and Maddie can show you the stables. You'll love the horses. Just watch out for Sadie and Vader." Camille shivered as if the names conjured unpleasant thoughts. "Micah can show you around the ranch tomorrow. I'm sure the two of you want some time to get to know each other."

Micah shook his head. "Sorry. I leave for Kansas City in the morning."

Haley tried not to react, but the news was like a kick in the stomach. She'd come here to get to know him, and he was leaving first thing.

"What? Why?" Camille asked.

"We're buying a new bull."

Camille waved her hand. "Send someone else."

"Hunter is going with me, but I have to go. There's a lot to do before we commit."

Exasperated, Camille huffed. "Haley drove a long way to see you."

Micah turned to Haley, but his gaze didn't hold hers for long. "I know. I'm sorry, but this is important for the future of the ranch. A bad bull can mess things up for years. I'll be back in a week or so."

Haley took a deep breath and turned up the corners of her mouth. "That's okay. I'll stay until you get back for sure."

"Well, someone needs to get you out of this house," Camille said. "I would show you around, but I have to work tomorrow. Plus, we're still on for decorating this weekend, right?"

"You know it," Haley agreed.

"Then Asher can keep you busy tomorrow," Mama Harding said. "Just tell him what you want to see, and he can show you."

Asher's head shot up, and he looked stunned. "But, I—"

Mama Harding held up a silencing hand that stopped his protest short. "Show her the best sights and make sure she gets all the photos she needs, then make sure she has fun. She's not just here for work."

"Yes, ma'am," Asher agreed.

Haley sat paralyzed, darting her glance to Asher and back to his mother. There must be an unwritten rule around here, and she reminded herself never to cross the matriarch.

Plus, *why* was the woman of the house insisting that Asher be her tour guide? Haley's cheeks burned at the possibility that Mama Harding might have seen the kiss.

When everyone had finished eating, the men relaxed and talked about the things they'd done today and the things they needed to do tomorrow. Micah rattled off a list of tasks that needed to be taken care of in his absence, and every man at the table accepted the list of duties with a nod.

Haley kept silent as they held their business meeting and only occasionally giggled at Levi making funny faces across the table.

Micah stood, and she rose to her feet beside him, eager to finally have time to talk.

"I didn't know you'd be leaving the ranch this week. I guess my timing is a little off."

Micah lifted one shoulder. "You couldn't have known."

"Tell me about it. There's always so much going on here. I'm surprised you ever had time to talk to me."

He finally gave her his full attention, and she noticed his eyes were green—much paler than her own.

Asher's eyes were a warm brown that reminded her of dark-brown sugar.

Why was she thinking about Asher's eyes?

"Yeah, I usually only have time to sneak away to the computer in the early mornings and late at night."

"I noticed," Haley said.

Micah cleared his throat. "Listen, I... um. It was nice chatting with you online, but I don't think I'm ready for anything more than that." He rubbed his neck. "I mean, I have to leave in the morning, and things are always busy here."

Haley's throat sank to the bottom of her stomach. "That's okay." She was lying. It wasn't okay. She was upset that things hadn't worked out with yet another man.

"The timing just isn't good right now."

"That's okay. I might still be here when you get back." She tried to smile, but she wasn't doing a very good job.

Micah gestured awkwardly toward the door. "Well, I need to get going. I have to pack tonight, and I need to meet Hunter when he gets back."

Haley's mood sank like a rock. Micah's rejection was the last straw in a long series of failures today.

"I'm really sorry about this. I—"

Haley interrupted. "You didn't do anything wrong. I don't want to keep you from your responsibilities."

"It's just a busy time right now, and I didn't know you were coming."

He was trying really hard to be nice, but she could also hear the reprimand in the undercurrent of his words. Apparently, spontaneity wasn't Micah's favorite attribute.

"I know. I should've talked to you about it. I thought it would be fun to surprise you." Haley wasn't a stranger to owning her mistakes. Living on the impulsive side often got her in hot water.

"I'm definitely surprised."

She caught a glimpse of Micah's smile. It was only a grin, but it was the first positive emotion he'd shown her. She was still getting used to thinking of him as Micah instead of the other brother from the photo, but he was definitely handsome. Too bad he'd dumped her before they'd even made it to relationship status.

In the photo Micah had sent her, he was the one standing with his arms crossed over his chest with a stern look on his face. Asher was the slightly taller brother with a smile so big and full of laughter that she could count most of the teeth in his mouth.

Maybe spending at least part of the day with Asher on the ranch tomorrow would brighten her mood. She hoped it wouldn't be awkward after that kiss. How had things gotten so mixed up?

"Well, I guess I'll see you at breakfast." Haley raised a hand for an awkward good-bye.

"Actually, I'll be leaving before sunup tomorrow."

She really wasn't going to catch a break. It was time to bow out and call it a day. "I'll just talk to you later. Have a safe trip."

"Thanks." Micah lifted his hand in a wave as he stepped away from her, out the door, and into the dark night.

Everyone else was still cleaning up the meeting room and thankfully not paying any attention to her. She raised her hands to her cheeks. They were burning up, and she would bet they were nice and red by now.

"Hey."

She jumped, startled by the greeting. "Asher, you scared me."

He tucked his hands behind his back and tilted his chin and his gaze down slightly. "I just wanted to let you know we can head out after breakfast in the morning."

"Okay. You don't have to be my tour guide if you don't want to. I can just hang out around here." After hearing his mother order him to cart her around, Haley wasn't feeling up to his charity.

"I really don't mind." His words were soft and held a ring of truth. Maybe it was because he'd made eye contact with her for the first time since she'd snapped that photo before supper. Maybe it was because he'd overheard Micah dismissing her. She hoped he hadn't.

"Be thinking about what you want to do, and let me know in the morning. Oh, and dress warm."

Well, that settled it. She'd go with Asher tomorrow, but she needed to spend the rest of the evening preparing herself to be next to the stranger she'd kissed earlier. "Okay. Thanks for this."

Asher lifted his chin, and a shadow of a grin tugged at his lips. "Anytime."

Haley spotted Mama Harding stepping out of

the kitchen and said, "I need to thank your mother for supper and then get to work." She pointed her thumb toward the stairs over her shoulder.

"See you in the morning."

"See you." Haley breathed deep and caught Mama Harding's attention. "Thanks for supper. It was delicious."

"You're welcome. We're having pancakes, bacon, and sausage in the morning."

Haley grinned. "Sounds good. I can't wait."

She waved a good night to a few others as she grabbed her camera and made her way up the stairs to her room. The open window looked out over the black void of the ranch, and she jerked the curtains closed. Backing away from the window, she counted down from five before swallowing and taking a deep breath.

Her mother's words played in Haley's head after every sunset.

The darkness can't hurt you.

CHAPTER 6
HALEY

Grabbing her laptop, she tucked it under her arm and quickly slid beneath the blankets on the bed. It was a trick she'd learned a long time ago —find an anchor, something to touch that was familiar.

With her laptop on, she could distract herself with work. She was most productive during the night hours when she was stuck inside. Distraction was another one of her favorite coping mechanisms.

The Blackwater Ranch website had one page with a few grainy photos. She opened a new document and began jotting down ideas. How could she capture the true ranch vibe they had going here? Some people would eat that up.

Meals with the family.

Seeing the rough and tough cowboys working the ranch.

Horseback riding.

Gorgeous scenery.

Peace and quiet.

The ideas continued to flow, and she began making notes on ways she could provide a visual that would convey the uplifting feeling she'd experienced that made her heart beat faster when she'd arrived.

It definitely wasn't Asher Harding.

Don't think about him. Focus on the ranch.

The longer she worked, the more her thoughts strayed to the stupid mistake she'd made when she kissed Asher. No, the mistake started when she came to Blackwater on a whim. Micah's dismissal had hurt way more than it should have. She wasn't a crier, but she found herself pushing back against that tickling in her throat and tingling in her nose that warned of the coming tears.

She sunk back into her work, trying to forget about the awful day. When she developed a headache from staring at the bright screen, she closed the laptop and dug her sketchbook out of her luggage. Slipping back into the bed, she closed her eyes and visualized the image in her mind.

When she opened her eyes and looked at the page, it was there—or it might as well be. She could complete a detailed sketch in a few hours. The tip of her pencil slid over the page like sand tumbling from one end of an hourglass to the other.

The outline of the face was giving her fits. Was it rounded or angular? She'd been so sure a moment ago, but now it was blurry in her mind.

She stopped with her pencil hovering over the outline of an eye. Was the iris dark or light? She tapped the point of her pencil on the rough edge of the eye, but she couldn't decide.

Grabbing the eraser, she scrubbed it over the top half of the sketch until the eyes and top of the head were gone. Then, she began sketching the hat— wide brimmed and tipped forward to cover the mysterious eyes.

An hour later, she sat looking at a completed sketch of a cowboy with his hat hanging low.

Whose face was beneath the hat?

She closed the sketchbook and tossed it into her suitcase. She'd had enough wonderings for one night, and the emotional turmoil was exhausting. Getting dumped was awful. Getting dumped before it even started was the worst.

"Let it Snow" played softly from her phone on the bedside table, and she sighed before reaching for it. A photo of her sister, Gabby, filled the screen.

She answered the call, ready to accept her reprimand today rather than let it seep into tomorrow. "Hello." Her tone was bland and hollow.

"Hey. You don't sound happy. Is everything okay?"

Haley swallowed hard and flopped onto her back on the bed. "No."

"What happened?" At least Gabby sounded concerned instead of disappointed.

"I met Micah. He isn't interested."

Gabby sighed. "I'm sorry, Hales."

"Me too," Haley whispered.

"Are you coming home?"

"Not yet. I promised them I would work on their website, which wouldn't take long if I had some decent photos. I'm supposed to get a tour of the ranch tomorrow."

"I know you were really excited about this trip, not only because of Micah, but because it sounded like a cool place."

"Well, he's leaving tomorrow. He'll be gone for a while."

"Then stay," Gabby said. "Have fun, and don't worry about relationships."

"Why am I so bad at love?" Haley whispered. A traitorous tear slid from the outer corner of her eye and across her temple into her hair. Some days, her heart felt so full of love that it would burst, and without a companion to share it with, it continued to pound on the walls of her chest, begging to be released.

"Listen closely, Haley. It's not love that you're bad at. It's patience. You're pushing something that should come in its own time."

Haley wiped the tear. "Why do I care so much that I can't find someone to love me?"

Gabby's voice was soft. "Lots of people love you."

"Romantically," Haley amended.

"I know how to fix this," Gabby said. "But you won't like it."

"Well, nothing I've done has worked so far. All I do is send men running for the hills."

"One of the things I love about you is that you're friendly. Please don't ever change that. But sometimes you're *too* friendly, and when you jump headlong into relationships, you're trying to have all the top of the mountain experiences at once. That's not how a real relationship works."

"I'm listening."

"Slow down," Gabby said.

"I feel like I've heard these words before."

"And I'll probably say them again. What I mean is, you need to stop looking and start listening."

"What am I trying to hear?" Haley asked.

"The Lord's plan."

Haley was silent for a moment as shame washed over her like a wave. "Okay."

"Will you try something for me? Take a break. Stop looking for love. Give yourself time to find out what the Lord has planned for you. Pray about it."

"Okay." Defeat and embarrassment settled

heavy around her. She should've listened to Gabby a long time ago.

She should've waited on the Lord.

"I promise you that a man will come into your life when it's time, but you have to stop chasing the things that aren't meant for you."

"I know."

"Take the month of December at least to pray about it."

"You mean swear off men for a month," Haley said.

"Pretty much. Focus on yourself and being happy alone. I think you need to master that before you jump into a commitment with someone anyway."

"It makes sense. I think you're right."

"I want you to be happy," Gabby whispered.

"I know. I love you."

"I love you, too, Hales."

She ended the call and did just what her sister advised. She prayed. And while she talked to God, she knew her sister was right. She needed to take about ten steps back and trust God's timing.

Grabbing the night-light from her bag, she plugged it in beside the bed, turned off the light, and slid back beneath the covers. Shadows stuck to the walls like life-size silhouettes, and she squeezed her eyes closed.

The darkness can't hurt you.

With an unsteady breath, she said a short prayer that the Lord would deliver her through another night.

She fitfully dreamed of a field of white with a black sky above it. Her heart raced as she scrambled for an anchor, but she was alone in the field. She crouched to place her palms on the ground, desperate for something to hold onto.

When she looked up, a man was standing in the snow, a cowboy hat shadowing his dark eyes.

She knew him. Where had she seen him before?

CHAPTER 7
ASHER

Asher woke early in the morning, before the sun, as usual, and rolled onto his back. He was a morning person, but he wasn't sure if he wanted to rush over to the main house or hide out in his cabin to avoid Haley today.

He wasn't the type to embarrass easily, but Haley had put him in a unique spot yesterday. Letting his arm rest over his eyes in the dark room, he prayed for the Lord to help him control his thoughts. He didn't want to be tangled up in a mess with Haley.

Why had he kissed her back?

Thinking about the kiss was the last thing he needed to be doing.

Prayer. He needed to pray more. If he was thinking about the Lord, he wasn't thinking about Haley.

He really needed to apologize to Micah and tell him about the kiss.

No kiss thoughts!

He flung the blankets off and sat on the side of the bed. Cradling his head in his hands, he tried praying again.

Lord, help me to fix this. I know I need to tell Micah, and I need to get a handle on my thoughts about Haley.

The kiss didn't mean anything. He needed to remember that. It wasn't intended for him. Her happiness and excitement were all for Micah.

Asher needed to tell Micah. He'd understand. It was a misunderstanding. He might even think it was funny.

Except Micah didn't have a humorous bone in his body.

Asher chuckled at his own joke. Yep, Micah definitely wouldn't think it was funny.

Asher needed a song. He began humming "Good Hearted Woman" by Waylon Jennings and was able to get through a shower and push the guilt aside.

He was still early to breakfast, and Haley was already in the meeting room helping his mother set up. Haley had taken his advice and dressed for the frigid weather. He could see a black undershirt beneath the collar of her thick, tan sweater. Her jeans were tucked into rugged, laced-up boots, and her dark-red hair fell in waves down her back.

Asher shook his head, thinking of the song that

would keep his mind off Haley. He hummed softly as he stepped up to his mom and relieved her of the stack of plates she carried.

"Morning, son." His mother leaned in and kissed his cheek.

"Morning, Ma."

Mama Harding returned to the kitchen, and he placed the dishes at the end of the serving counter. He remembered the tune again and resumed humming. He needed to get used to being around Haley if they were going to be spending the day together.

"Is that 'Good Hearted Woman?'" Haley asked.

Asher halted his hum and turned his attention to her, surprised she would recognize the old song. "Yeah. You like it?"

"Waylon is a classic. My mom is from Alabama, and she always listened to the good ones." Haley turned back toward the serving counter and tilted her head to the side. "She said it reminded her of her daddy. I never got to meet him, but Mom always talks about him like he was her hero."

Asher tucked his chin and took a step to the side, closer to her. "My parents talk about my granddad that way. I've heard some crazy stories about him, but they always tell them with a smile."

Haley grinned. "Do you like having a big family?"

"Yeah. What's not to like? I'm lucky they haven't voted me off the island yet."

"They say if you can't point out the crazy one, it's probably you."

Asher nodded emphatically. "Definitely Lucas."

Haley laughed, and Asher tried not to look at her. He really tried, but he loved seeing people laugh. Her shoulders bounced, and she covered her mouth with the back of her hand. It didn't hide anything. He could see the joy in her eyes.

Asher cleared his throat. "I'll go see if Mama needs help in the kitchen." He left in a hurry before Haley could say anything and burst into the quiet kitchen.

His mom was pulling jelly jars out of the refrigerator. "Can you take these?"

He took the jars and walked back out into the meeting room. Haley was standing in the same place, but she'd turned around to lean her back against the serving counter.

Asher stepped around her to put the condiments on the far end of the serving counter.

A familiar hum started deep and began to grow. It was Haley, and Asher bit his lips between his teeth.

This was a game he could win.

"Crazy," he said.

"Hmm. You're good. I'll have to up my game. Everyone knows Patsy Cline."

He wasn't sure if he wanted to run away or hug her right now. She was trying to calm his nerves with a game, and he said a silent thanks to the Lord for making this easier.

Asher took a deep breath and faced her. "Listen, should we—"

"Nope," she interrupted. "We definitely should not talk about yesterday."

Asher held up his hands. "Sounds good to me."

There was a moment of silence before Haley whipped her attention to him. "Why did you kiss me back if you didn't know who I was?"

"You said no kiss talk!"

"Shh. You want to keep your voice down, cowboy?" Haley whisper-screamed.

"Sorry." Asher bared his teeth in an apologetic grimace. He shrugged. "I could ask you the same thing."

She laughed, and then looked at him expectantly, waiting for a real answer.

Asher brushed his hand over the nape of his neck. "I don't really have an excuse."

"Don't give me an excuse," she said. "Tell me the truth, please. I'm trying to make sense of this."

"That makes two of us." He sighed and faced her. "The easy answer is that a woman ran up to me and kissed me like I was the only man in the world that mattered." He turned to face the stack of plates on the counter, too afraid to face her when he confessed. "I want to be that man for someone, and I got caught up in the moment. I'm sorry for the mess I put you in."

Haley shook her head. "You didn't do that. It was my fault. I guess it doesn't matter much now. I wanted to surprise Micah, but I ended up surprising you instead."

Asher faced her with a smirk. "I'm going to have to ask you not to surprise me ever again. My conscience can't handle secrets."

"It's a deal." Haley stuck out her hand to shake on it.

Asher grabbed her hand and gave it one firm shake before they both transitioned into a fist bump and an explosion at the end.

He narrowed his eyes at her. "Stop reading my mind."

Haley smiled and nodded. "Got it."

Asher scanned the room, willing everyone in his family to get their lazy bones out of bed so he could eat breakfast. "So, you came here on a whim to meet a man you hardly know?"

Haley grinned. "Pretty much. I wanted to get to know him. When he mentioned the ranch, I looked it up." She lifted her hands out to the sides, palms up. "It looked like a cute place to get some work done before Christmas, and I assumed I'd spend some time with Micah and get to know him. Looks like I was wrong about that."

"Wow. You were going to kiss a man you hardly knew?" Asher asked.

Haley lifted a finger. "Correction. I *did* kiss a man I hardly knew."

Asher felt his face grow warm. "You certainly did. That's crazy."

"Did you just call me crazy? The word you're looking for is spontaneous."

It was fun watching her defend her impulsive decision, and he grinned. "You're crazy."

"Crazy is in the eye of the beholder."

Asher whispered, "Crazy."

Haley leaned in and whispered, "Adventurous."

He shook his head and tried to keep the smile from his face. "You certainly have a positive attitude and a way with words."

"I should. I've been writing since I was a kid."

Asher tilted his head. "What do you write?"

"Everything." Haley's smile grew, and her green eyes were bright. "Poetry, short stories, songs—"

"You write songs?" Asher asked.

"And sing them."

"No way. I do too."

Haley gaped, but her smile still fought to turn her lips up at the corners. "We're samesies!"

Asher shook his head. "We are not samesies. I don't even know what that means."

"I said we're samesies. I want to hear your songs."

The excitement Asher often felt whenever music worked its way into his life grew in his middle. "You'll have to come hear me play."

"Where?"

"Barn Sour. It's a little hole in the wall place in town."

The door opened, and Asher and Haley both turned to see who had arrived. Lucas and Maddie left their hats and coats at the door before he rested his arm around her shoulders.

Mama Harding stepped out of the kitchen. "Aaron called. He's having breakfast with Levi at his place. They had a long night. Your dad decided to skip."

Lucas clapped his hands together. "So, this is it. Let's eat!"

Haley turned to him with wide eyes. "Skip breakfast? *That's* what's crazy. It's my favorite meal."

Asher wasn't sure what to make of her joke. He didn't have a problem laughing at himself, but many others did. Seeing Haley embrace the crazy label eased the nervousness swirling in his middle. "It's my favorite meal too."

She narrowed her eyes at him. "What's your stance on frozen pizzas?"

"Yes to the cheap ones. Pass on the big fancy ones."

Haley patted his shoulder and said, "We're going

to get along just fine, friend," before stepping away from him to greet Maddie.

Asher's breathing grew shallow at her declaration. He wasn't afraid they'd end up at odds. He was worried they would get along too well.

CHAPTER 8
ASHER

Breakfast wasn't as awkward as Asher had expected after Haley broke the ice. He was able to relax while everyone else got to know Haley. With half of the family missing, the mealtime chatter was more reserved than usual.

After breakfast, Asher caught her attention and jerked his chin toward the door. Haley practically skipped across the room, waving her good-byes to everyone.

"So, what are we doing today?" she asked.

"That's up to you. We probably won't be out all day, unless you're comfortable with the freezing temperature."

"I dressed for the job today." She slid her arms into a thick coat.

Asher grabbed his hat and corduroy coat as Haley lifted her long hair from the collar of hers. The light hit the coppery color just right, making it shine.

"Mom said this isn't all about the website. You're expected to have fun too."

Haley dismissed him with a flick of her hand before picking up her camera bag. "That'll be easy. I always have fun."

Asher could relate to that mindset. Working the ranch every day could get boring, but he found ways to mix things up for him and his brothers. It helped that the weather usually threw them a curveball. Days like today when the air was freezing but the sky was blue called for an optimistic mindset.

They stepped out onto the porch where Dixie acknowledged them with a sharp bark.

Haley squatted to greet the border collie. "Who is this?"

"This is Dixie. She runs the place."

Haley puckered her lips and scratched Dixie's jaws. "I bet you do, pretty girl. Do you boss these men around?"

Asher propped against the wooden column on the porch to give Haley some time to play with the dog. Dixie got a lot of attention, but she was always looking for more.

Asher leaned down to brush the sprinkling of snow from Dixie's back. "She can come with us today."

Haley tilted her head to the dog and said, "Will

you show me around the ranch? I bet you know all the best places."

"To her, the best place is right here at the main house. Levi sneaks breakfast to her most mornings."

Haley laughed and whispered to Dixie, "I knew we liked that kid."

"Let's load up," Asher said as he stepped off the porch. He opened the passenger door for Haley and waited until she was settled in her seat before closing the door. He lowered the tailgate of his truck and patted the bed for Dixie to jump in.

When he slid into the driver's seat, he started the truck and bumped up the heat. "You're welcome to adjust the temperature however you want. There are lots of things we can see without getting out."

She leaned forward and studied the buttons and knobs of the old truck. Instead of changing the heat settings, she turned on the radio.

Asher stayed quiet as she skimmed the programmed channels. They were all his favorites—90s country, bluegrass, 80s rock, and modern Christian music.

She pressed the third button and listened for a moment before turning the volume down and leaning back in her seat. "You like this one?"

Asher nodded to the beat of the Brooks & Dunn song. "Yeah. You like 90s country?"

Haley pressed the buttons on her camera. "My

mom always listened to it when we were growing up."

"We?"

"I have five siblings."

"Wow. And I thought I had a big family," Asher said.

"You do, and I love it. Supper last night reminded me of home. I like being around a lot of people. I get lonely by myself."

The song changed to "Right Where I Need to Be" by Gary Allen, and Haley rested her head back and turned to look out the window. "I like this one too. What's your favorite music genre?"

Asher thought for a moment. "There isn't much I don't like when it comes to music."

"So you're an R&B lover?" She turned to him with a taunting grin.

"Not R&B. I'm not a fan of Pop either," he said.

Haley nodded. "Same, but I don't like jazz or classical music. Does that make me unrefined?"

Asher bit the inside of his lip to contain a smile. "Yeah. I could do without those too. We're just a couple of uncultured swine." They topped the low rise at the stable and he nodded to the building. "We'll stop by here later. I have a feeling Lucas and Maddie are going to monopolize your time."

"So they take care of the horses?" Haley asked.

"Technically, that's just Maddie's job. We had to hire her a few months ago to help out. Lucas is the best with the horses, but he has a lot on his plate. We needed someone with his knowledge and the time to devote to them. Horses are just as important as the cattle."

"I haven't seen a single cow. Are you sure this is a ranch?" Haley asked.

"Everything we do is about the cattle. That's why Micah is driving to another state to get a new bull. We have to rotate them every so often. The bull is half of your herd."

Haley grinned. "I learned something new today. Thanks, teach."

Asher winked. "Stick with me, and I'll teach you a thing or two."

"So what else is there to see here?"

Asher rested his wrist on the steering wheel and settled back into his seat. "A lot of wide open spaces. There are two creeks that line the northern and eastern borders. I really need to check the water for the herd. We keep it moving, but sometimes it freezes anyway when it gets this cold."

"Seeing a real live cow is on my list of things to do while I'm here," Haley said.

Asher narrowed his eyes at her. "Are you saying you've never seen a cow before?"

"Pretty much. I mean, I've seen them in fields on the side of the road, but not up close and personal."

"Time to change that." He set a course for the north pasture where the herd was currently located.

Haley scanned the white fields as he drove, and Asher made a point not to look her way. That red hair was bright against the colorless landscape, but those eyes were distracting. He needed to focus on something other than the excited woman sitting next to him.

The next song came on and he hummed the tune. Within seconds, she joined in, adding a sweet note to the wordless song.

"Am I going to get to hear you sing?" he asked.

Haley narrowed her eyes and bit her bottom lip. "Am I going to get to hear *you* sing?"

"Hunter and I play at Barn Sour a lot. He's not one for singing, so it usually falls to me."

Haley sat up straighter. "I want to go."

"Sure. We're playing next weekend if they're back by then. You should come. Camille and Maddie are usually there."

When the herd came into view, Haley scooted to the edge of her seat to peer out. "They're everywhere!"

Asher chuckled. "That's the point of a ranch."

Haley opened her door and eagerly jumped out. Asher shook his head and grabbed a crowbar from the back seat. She was already snapping photos when he rounded the truck. He left her to her work while he broke up the ice in the trough and water system. Dixie ran around Haley's legs, curious about the stranger in the field. When he finished breaking up the ice, he propped against the truck and waited for Haley.

A minute later, she noticed him and made her way back to the truck with a pep in her step. Her boots crunched the snow all the way to him.

"You don't have to rush. I can wait," Asher said.

"I'm finished. Let's see something else."

There were a handful of other troughs to break up, and Haley captured photos each time they stopped. At the last trough, Asher noticed her scanning the area as if she were looking for something.

"Can I help you with something?" he asked.

"I want to get a shot from somewhere higher. I'm in a valley here."

Asher waved her over. He linked his fingers and held them low for her to step into. "Climb on the roof."

"Of your truck? Are you sure?"

"I don't think you'll hurt this old thing. It's the highest point around here."

Haley let her camera dangle around her neck and braced her hands on the rusty hood of the old pickup. She rested her boot in his hands and tested her weight.

"Are you afraid of heights?" Asher questioned.

"No, I'm afraid of the dark." She admitted the fear casually, and it was impossible to know if she was sincere.

"You don't trust me to hold you?" he asked.

"I do." She pushed up on the foot in his hands and climbed onto the hood. When she stood, the wind caught her hair, and she turned in all directions scanning the scene. "Wow. I can see everything from here."

Asher turned away from her and breathed in the cold wind. Getting caught staring at her was the last thing he needed. He propped his back against the truck and waited for her to finish.

"Okay. I think I have what I need. This was a good idea." She crouched to make her way down from the top of the truck like a spider.

Asher met her at the front to help her down. He wasn't sure how he could lift her down with the least amount of physical contact, but when she extended her hands to brace on his shoulders, he took her lead and grabbed her waist to gently ease her to the ground.

When she was steady, he released his hold on her. Touching Haley was not a good idea. "So, are you ready to head back? I can get you settled in with Lucas and Maddie before lunch."

"Sounds good. I want to see the rivers, but we can do that some other time."

Haley scrolled through the photos she'd taken as they drove back to the stables, and Asher resisted the urge to turn on the radio. He needed something in his head to erase the vision of Haley standing on the roof of his truck.

When he parked in front of the stables, Haley jumped out of the truck, ready to meet the horses.

Asher opened the door of the truck, letting in the rush of winter. "Let's find Lucas and Maddie and get you saddled up."

CHAPTER 9
HALEY

Haley breathed in the cold air and formed her mouth into an O to push it out. The morning with Asher hadn't been as awkward as she'd expected. At least they could laugh about the kiss now.

She was still bummed about Micah. She came here to get to know him, and he'd cut her loose within hours of her arrival.

It shouldn't bother her that Micah hadn't asked for her phone number before he left. If he knew enough to cut her loose, he wasn't the one for her.

Meeting him last night had been a huge letdown. He'd been respectful and sweet when they were chatting, but Haley needed more than that in a relationship. She needed a companion, someone who would stand beside her through life and be her best friend—definitely not someone who had luke-warm feelings for her.

She'd made the long drive up here because Micah had been the first match on the Fated Mates site who had shown any real interest in her. She'd scared a dozen others off with her eagerness. But Micah had asked questions to get to know her, and she'd been truly interested in his life on the ranch. They'd hit it off, and she'd felt they were compatible. But only hearing from him twice a day for a few minutes each time wasn't enough to get to know someone. Then she'd had the bright idea to visit, and the whole plan had backfired on her.

Asher opened the door to the stables and moved to the side for her to enter first. Getting her thoughts straight about Micah was hard when she'd spent so much time thinking that Asher was Micah. That photograph had caused a lot of confusion. She knew which was which now, but she'd spent almost a month thinking that the image of Asher was the one she was chatting with online. To her muddled mind, Asher was the man she'd come to meet.

She needed to start training herself to think that Asher was just another one of the Harding brothers. She would look at Asher and tell herself, *That isn't Micah. He's not the one you came here to get to know.*

Asher closed the door behind them and caught up with her. She snuck a glance at him walking tall and proud beside her. The traitorous memories of that kiss seeped into her thoughts, and she snapped her attention to the other end of the stables. *No relationships*, she reminded herself. Gabby had given her good advice, and she intended to stick to it. Plus, Asher was turning into a pretty good friend now that they'd worked past the initial shock.

Haley scanned the quiet stables. "I don't think they're here."

"They are," Asher said. "I bet they're in the tack room."

She followed Asher to a room on the far side of the stables. Lucas and Maddie greeted them with welcoming smiles.

Maddie wiped her brow on the sleeve of her shirt. "Hey. We didn't expect you today. We're reorganizing the tack room."

Asher leaned against the doorframe and crossed his arms. "I'm just showing Haley around. You think she could get a ride tomorrow?"

"Of course," Maddie said.

"I don't want to impose," Haley added. "I know you have other things to do."

Lucas rested a saddle on one of the metal poles sticking out of the wall. "It's not a problem. We need to exercise the horses anyway. I'll bring in Skittle and Sprite for you to meet in the morning."

Haley's grin bloomed. "Skittle and Sprite. Who gets to name the horses?"

Maddie leaned against a wall to rest. "Sometimes, if it's a bought horse, it already has a name. If it's born here on the ranch, we get to name it."

"Yeah, Levi named Skittle after his favorite candy," Asher said.

Haley chuckled. "I love that kid."

Asher quirked up one side of his mouth in a grin. "He's a handful, but none of us remember life without him."

It seemed Asher had a soft spot for his nephew. If a man liked dogs and kids, it usually meant they were playful and friendly. "So, would you mind telling me about all these things? I know less than nothing about horses."

Maddie jumped into an enthusiastic explanation of every piece of equipment and what it was used for. Asher and Lucas added their own bits of wisdom, and between the three of them, she'd gotten a crash course on horses that felt like drinking from a fire hose.

When it was time for lunch, she hopped back in the truck with Asher. "That was awesome."

"Horses are cool. Well, I'm not sure I've met an animal that wasn't cool. Except maybe a spider."

Haley tucked her lips between her teeth to hide her grin. "What? Are you afraid of spiders?"

"One hundred percent. There was one time when I was pumping gas, and a spider fell on my hand. I lost my mind and sprayed gas everywhere."

Haley released her laugh. "You're kidding!"

"I wish. I banged my knee on the side of the truck, and it hasn't been the same since." He rubbed the area in question as if the mere thought conjured pain.

"That is the best thing I've heard all day."

"It's not very funny to me!" Asher said. "I can never show my face at that gas station again."

Haley covered her mouth and continued to chuckle.

"Let it all out. Ha, ha, ha," Asher said.

She finally suppressed her giggles and snuck a side glance at him. Thankfully, he was smiling too. At least his fear was comical. She couldn't say the same for her own.

Asher began humming a tune. It was familiar, and the words jumped from her mouth. "'9 to 5' by Dolly Parton."

"You're good at this game," Asher said as he shifted. "'9 to 5' isn't something I'm actually familiar with. The ranch dictates our hours."

"Me either. I'm a freelance web designer, so I work when there's work to be done. I work best at night though, and it frees up a lot of my time during the day."

Asher glanced at her before looking back at the gravel path they followed. "What do you like to do?"

The question was broad, and she smiled as she thought of the ways she could answer. "I like to create. I like to write. I sketch a lot, but I like to paint if I have time and space to work on a big project."

Asher's eyes opened wide. "That covers a lot of the art spectrum. What kind of songs do you write?"

Of course, Asher would be interested in the songs. "Usually love songs. I'm a reckless romantic. That's the opposite of a hopeless romantic, in case you were wondering."

"A reckless romantic? Sounds wild and dangerous," Asher said. "I guess that's how you end up kissing strangers."

Haley lifted a finger in the air between them. "No talking about erroneous kisses."

"Yes, ma'am. What are you writing now?"

Haley sighed. "I'm kind of stuck on one. I haven't had any inspiration."

Asher narrowed his gaze at her. "Are you saying my kiss wasn't inspiring? I'm crushed."

Haley giggled and slapped her leg. "I said no talking about the kiss!"

"Okay, I'll be good." Asher composed himself. "Why aren't you inspired?"

"I had a boyfriend for a long time—well, it was like six months—and I thought we would get married. He didn't think so." Haley turned her attention back to the window as they pulled up at the main house. "I've just had a bad run at relationships lately."

Her creative block had more to do with her

worries that she wasn't cut out for marriage. What if God had a plan for her that required she remain single her whole life? The thought sent a chill down her spine that had nothing to do with the frigid weather in Blackwater.

Maybe she was just bad at love. At this point, with two dozen failed relationships under her belt, she needed to consider the possibility that *she* was the problem, not them. Gabby's advice sounded better and better each time she thought about it.

Asher parked the truck and rested back in his seat. "Maybe Micah will put an end to that."

Haley didn't confirm or deny Asher's assumption. She stayed quiet and hoped he'd let the subject die.

He patted her shoulder. "Chin up. It'll all work out."

Haley got out of the truck before Asher could open the door for her. "I think I have enough pictures to get started on the website after lunch."

"Good. It was nice hanging out with you today," Asher said.

"Yeah, you too." It was exponentially better than sitting in her room all day, and she liked having someone to joke around with. Her initial plan for this trip hadn't worked out, but at least she'd made some friends at Blackwater Ranch.

CHAPTER 10
ASHER

The next morning, Asher woke before the sun and arrived early for breakfast. Sitting around in his quiet cabin wouldn't work. He was an early riser, and the least he could do was see if Mama needed help in the kitchen.

The sky was still dark when he pulled up at the main house, but light shone through every window of the bottom floor of the old, wooden house as if someone had lit a candle in a lantern.

He stepped into the meeting room and shivered as the warmth hit his skin. Haley sat alone at the table with a laptop in front of her. Her dark-red hair was a stark contrast to her tan sweater.

Haley stretched her arms above her head. "Good morning, sunshine."

"Morning. No sunshine yet," Asher said.

Haley glanced at the window that framed a

black scene. "I wanted to show your parents the adjustments I made to the website last night. I'm hoping to get some good photos of the horses today."

"Can I see?"

When Haley waved him over, he stepped up behind her and propped a hand on the table next to her computer. Her hair smelled like coconut and sunshine, and he shook his head. Girly smells were few and far between on the ranch, and the scent caught him off guard.

"This is what I have for the home page. This part isn't finished yet. I left space for images here. The booking page is up, but the links don't work. Your mom let me into the other guest rooms yesterday evening so I could get some photos."

"I never saw the website we had before, but this looks great." He pointed to the header at the top. "Is that a logo?"

"Yeah. Do you already have one? I just threw this one together."

Asher studied the horseshoe, open at the top with Blackwater Ranch written over it. "We don't have one. That's so cool."

"I threw this one together, too, so you could choose." She pulled up another tab on her laptop to show him a bold, backward B that rested against an R in the center of an oval.

"Wow. I like both of them. You choose."

Haley softly sang "Should've Been a Cowboy" by Toby Keith as she clicked and moved things around on the screen in front of her, lost in her work. She had musical talent for sure.

Asher turned his head slightly and saw her chewing on her bottom lip as she worked. When his heart began racing, he stood to his full height and took a step back. He liked being around Haley, but he needed to remember that she wasn't here to goof off with him. She was here for Micah.

Asher met his mother in the kitchen and gladly accepted orders from her as they prepared for breakfast. Sunrise was after seven in the morning now, and Levi burst into the room with enough energy to fuel the entire Harding family for the day.

Asher caught his nephew in a hug and squeezed while the boy wiggled in delight.

When Levi was back on his feet, he bounced on his toes. "Guess what? I already had breakfast. Dad let me have cereal!"

Asher knelt to Levi's height and narrowed his eyes. "Was it the good kind?"

"Froot Loops!"

Asher sighed. "I'm jealous. Froot Loops are the best." He tousled Levi's hair. "I want to be like you when I grow up."

Levi laughed. "You *are* grown up."

"Who told you that? Lies!"

"My daddy. He said I have to mind you because you're old."

"I'm not old! Your dad doesn't know what he's talking about."

Levi put his hands on his hips. "Yes, he does. He knows everything."

Asher leaned in and pretended to whisper to Levi. "Don't tell him I said this, but he ain't pretty to look at, his feet smell, and his ears are crooked."

Asher and Levi both looked up when they heard chuckling. Camille and Haley stood behind Asher, covering their mouths to stifle the laughter.

He wished Haley would let the happy sound escape, but perhaps he liked it too much when she looked at him with a smile that could light up the night.

Camille reached for Levi's hand. "Come on, troublemaker. You need to wash up."

By the time Lucas, Maddie, and Noah arrived, the meeting room was bustling with energy. Everyone washed up and helped Mama Harding bring in the rest of the breakfast trays.

Asher fell into line and ended up at the table between Levi and Camille. Lucas and Maddie monopolized Haley's conversation as they peppered her with tips and things to remember about the horses before her ride this morning.

When everyone had finished eating, Silas took over the morning duties list. After his heart attack a few years ago, their dad stepped back from the daily grind and opted to spend more time with their mother. The brothers agreed the old man had worked a lifetime of backbreaking days and deserved the rest, but he was ready to resume his old job as ranch manager in Micah's absence.

Asher volunteered for more than his fair share of duties for the day. If he played his cards right, he could skip lunch and stay busy until suppertime. Everyone needed a solid day of hard work every now and then, and he liked knowing there wasn't anything left unfinished at the end of the day.

When the meeting was over, Asher calculated his mental to-do list and found that it would take up every daylight hour to complete. Even with that reassurance, he hung back to help clean up. He kept his head down and wiped the table as Lucas, Maddie, and Haley walked past. The whistled tune of George Strait's "Blue Clear Sky" grabbed his attention and demanded he acknowledge the game he played with Haley.

She was already halfway to the door when she looked over her shoulder. The lyrics seemed to roll over his tongue, begging to be sung, but he swallowed the urge. Instead, he set his sights on the kitchen. He wasn't too fond of the way his pulse raced when she did something cool like hum his favorite song, and he was beginning to worry he liked their easy friendship too much.

Just keep walking. Put her out of your head and pretend that she doesn't like the same things you do. Pretend she doesn't set your skin on fire when she looks at you.

He closed the kitchen door behind him and wiped his sweaty hands on the rag before throwing it into the laundry basket. He could be friends with Haley. She was only here until Christmas anyway. It would've been a lot easier if she hadn't kissed him, then played games with tunes, and looked so happy standing on the roof of his truck admiring his home.

He was getting in over his head. He had a long to-do list today, and keeping any thoughts of Haley strictly platonic was at the top.

His mother rounded the corner into the kitchen. "What are you still doing here? You better get going."

"Yes, ma'am." He turned to walk out the way he'd come in.

"I hope you'll come in for lunch. Haley told me she likes baked chicken."

Asher stilled at the mention of her name. "You sure are going out of your way to make sure she's happy. I doubt she'll give us a bad review."

His mother looked at him as if she'd never seen the man standing before her. "The Lord's Word says we may be entertaining angels when we have a stranger under our roof."

Asher was familiar with the passage in the book

of Hebrews, and he was certain his mother had always treated others as if they were sent from the Lord. He was ashamed for questioning his mother's goodness.

Asher nodded and had one foot out the door when his mother made her last point.

"You'd do well to treat her the same. She's certainly a gift."

As much as Asher wanted to disagree, he couldn't. Not when he was sure his mother was right about Haley Meadows.

CHAPTER 11
HALEY

Haley rode with Maddie and Lucas to the stables after breakfast, and Dixie ran along beside the truck. Who knew there was so much to caring for horses? Haley had a million questions.

When they arrived at the stables, Lucas unlocked the gate and trudged through the light snow toward a nearby horse.

"Does he really have to go get the horse? Can't you just call them?" Haley asked.

Maddie chuckled. "Some will come without having to be called. Dolly does that, but she's already in the stables. Sprite and Skittle are a little stubborn and make us work for it."

Haley and Maddie talked while Lucas led Skittle in from the field.

"It's too cold to ride for long, so we'll spend the

morning feeding and grooming and ride after lunch," Maddie explained.

Inside the stables, small heaters and fans were situated in front of each stall, and Lucas led Skittle to an open bay on the far end while Maddie explained how they fed the horses. A large white board hung on the wall in the feed room where metal cans with lids were labeled for different feeds. A chart with names, times, feeds, and supplements filled every space of the board. They gathered feed for the first horse, and Maddie introduced Haley to Dolly.

"This is my baby," Maddie crooned as she stroked the horse's copper mane. "She's about ten years old, and I've had her since I was sixteen. We used to barrel race. She's a quarter horse, so we've been training her to help with the herding."

Once they'd fed the horses, Lucas walked Haley through the steps for grooming. There were various brushes, combs, picks, and ointments involved, and Haley's head was spinning when it came time to learn to put on the saddle.

It took them hours to complete all of the basic grooming and care for the horses, especially since everything was slowed for Haley to understand. Before they'd finished grooming all the horses, it was lunchtime.

Haley wasn't sure how she'd worked up an appetite so quickly, but her stomach growled on the way to the main house. She laid a hand on her stomach and laughed. "Sorry. I think I did too much talking and not enough eating this morning."

Maddie nodded. "Working with the horses will wear you out, especially if someone gets stubborn and puts up a fight. Training a horse requires patience."

"Oops. Might not be the best career for me then. I'm on the flighty side," Haley joked.

"My childhood was a series of surprises, so I like being grounded here. I like knowing the horses depend on me." Maddie smiled. "And getting to work with Lucas is a plus."

"You two are so cute together."

"He had to be patient with me too. I was stubborn, but I came around. I'm glad I did because the Hardings are the best thing that's happened to me since my aunt took me in."

"Wait. What happened to your parents?" Haley asked.

They were pulling up at the main house, and Maddie waved a dismissive hand in the air. "It's a long story, and it's a drag. Maybe some other time. Today is about fun."

Maddie jumped out of the truck as soon as she killed the engine, and Haley followed, jogging toward the warmth that awaited inside the main house. A roaring chatter filled the meeting room when the family started filing in. Haley got sucked into one conversation that bled into another and another. The constant stream of chatter and laughter filled her with a familiar warmth.

When Mama Harding ushered Haley to the front of the line, she looked around the room. "Where's Asher?"

"He had about three jobs too many today. I expect we won't see him until supper," Mama said.

Haley tried to squash the tiny spark of disappointment. She was getting used to joking around with Asher. She'd had a great time today, and she was eager to tell him about it.

After lunch, Haley, Lucas, and Maddie went back to the stables. Lucas led some of the horses around so Haley could photograph them, then she was able to get some nice photos of Maddie riding. Haley was a silent observer for the next few hours while the trainers worked, and she had hundreds of images to choose from by three in the afternoon.

Haley was scrolling through the last round of images on her camera when Maddie led Sprite out of the stables. "You ready to ride?"

"Sure. Just let me drop this off inside," Haley said.

"Put it in the office. It's the first door on the right."

Haley tucked her camera into a chair and jogged to meet Lucas, Maddie, and the horses outside.

Maddie went over some basic riding commands, and Haley nodded along.

Lucas met them with a bulky tiered block. "I know you can do it on your own, but it's easier on the horse's back if you use a mounting block."

Haley grinned. "I'll never refuse a little extra help. So, I just put my foot here and swing over?"

Maddie grabbed the bottom of Sprite's mane. "Yeah. Just grab here and the back of the saddle there and swing your leg over."

Haley focused on each of the commands. *Grab, grab, lift, swing.* Except when she tried to execute them all at the same time, she forgot to balance and ended up wobbling in the air for a tense second before plopping into the seat a little skewed and with an *oof.*

Lucas raised a fist to his mouth to hide his laughter. "So much for going easy on the horse's back."

Haley dramatically flipped her hair, but most of it was caught in her scarf. "Not everyone can fall onto a horse." She tried to adjust her seating, but the horse moved whenever she squirmed.

"Now, click your tongue and say 'go,'" Maddie said. "She needs a command to go with the sound, so make sure you don't just cluck at her."

Sprite moved into a slow walk as Haley gave the order, and she settled into a rhythm. Maddie demonstrated how to turn the horse and gave Haley a few other commands to use. They didn't venture far from the stables, but Haley and Sprite were both beginning to sweat despite the freezing temperatures.

When they were closed back inside the stable, Lucas and Maddie showed Haley how to groom the horses after riding. The process was much like the early-morning grooming, but the explanations went swifter now that Haley was familiar with the activity. They let the horses cool down and started closing up the stables for the day.

The stable door creaked open, and everyone turned to see Camille walking in. "Hey, I need to steal Haley from you."

Maddie waved a dismissing hand. "She's all yours."

"I'll catch up with you at supper," Haley said before following Camille out. "What's up?"

"There's a surprise waiting for you at the main house." Camille winked.

"Is it my lap desk? I ordered it a few days ago."

Camille shook her head. "Not a what. It's a who."

Haley picked up the pace. It had to be Micah. Could he have gotten back so soon? She hadn't told Camille—or anyone—about Micah's premature breakup before he left. Haley slid into the passenger seat and squirmed the whole way to the main house. When Camille shifted into park, Haley reluctantly stepped out of the truck. She wasn't sure if she really wanted to see him now, and her new pact to let relationships happen in God's time was at the forefront of her mind. She followed Camille up the porch steps and stopped when she remembered to take off her dirty boots. She precariously balanced on one foot as she tugged her boots off and stepped into the warm meeting room.

Where was Micah? The cavernous room was empty.

Camille walked in, and Haley turned to ask about Micah when she heard a familiar voice.

"Hales!"

Haley's eldest sister, Beth, clomped down the stairs in her tasseled booties. Her strawberry-blonde hair hung straight and loose over her shoulders, framing her youthful face.

Excitement and relief swirled in Haley's stomach. "Hey! What are you doing here?" She ran to meet her sister and wrap her in a hug.

"You didn't answer any of my calls or messages! Jess said she talked to you, and you were having the best time. I wanted to get in on the fun and spend some time with you."

Haley pulled out of the hug and smiled at Beth. "I'm glad you're here. How did you even find it?"

"I did a lot of Googling, but Gabby said you told her a woman made your booking over the phone.

When I called here, Anita answered the phone and confirmed that I had the right place."

"How long are you staying?"

Beth shrugged. "At least through the weekend. I still have some Christmas shopping to do when I get home."

Camille stepped up beside them, and Haley bumped shoulders with her new friend. "Beth, this is Camille. Camille, this is my sister, Beth."

"Welcome to Blackwater," Camille said. "We're glad to have you."

"Thanks. I was just unpacking. I'll be back down in a little bit, and we can decide what to do tonight." Beth turned and jogged back up the stairs, clomping with every footfall.

When Beth was out of sight, Camille grinned. "Does she know Blackwater doesn't have late-night entertainment?"

They both chuckled. "I don't think so. She might not stay through the weekend."

Camille shrugged. "At least the Christmas parade is tomorrow night. That should be fun."

Haley twisted her mouth to the side. She'd been hoping to see the Christmas parade, but not if it was after dark. This weekend might not be much fun for her either.

CHAPTER 12

ASHER

Asher hadn't finished up his work before dark, and by that time, he was too exhausted to eat. He'd driven right past the main house to his cabin and fallen into the bed in his work clothes.

The bright side of going to bed early was waking up refreshed. His back was stiff, but the hot shower washed away his aches and pains. He was dressed and walking into the main house before the sun peeked over the distant Big Horn Mountains. It wasn't a surprise that he was the first one up, but he was always happy to help Mom and Dad get breakfast ready.

His mother greeted him with a kiss on the cheek and a bowl of white gravy to take to the serving counter. The rest of the Hardings and ranch workers, including Jameson, made their way in shortly after sunrise. By the time the last of the meal was placed on the serving counter, Asher was looking for Haley. She wouldn't miss breakfast.

No sooner than he'd finished his scan of the meeting room, Haley made her way down the stairs with another woman beside her who had long, strawberry-blonde hair.

Haley clomped into the room in her low-heeled boots. "Sorry we're late. Sleepyhead didn't want to wake up." She smiled and pointed her thumb over her shoulder at the other woman.

The bright-eyed stranger zeroed in on Asher. "Hey. I don't think I met you last night." She stuck her hand out but kept it tucked close to her middle so he would have to move closer to grasp it.

"Asher Harding. You must be a new guest." He shook her hand. "Sorry I didn't make it to supper last night."

"I'm Beth. Haley's sister." She tucked a strand of her straight hair behind her ear and kept her gaze locked on him. She also kept her grip on his hand.

"Wow. Haley told me she had sisters, but I didn't know you'd be visiting too. Welcome to Blackwater Ranch." He tugged on his hand when it began to sweat, and she relinquished it.

"Thanks," Beth said.

Haley tugged her sister's arm. "They're waiting for us."

"Why?"

"Guests are served first."

"Oh," Beth grinned at Asher. "Save me a seat?"

"Sure." He wasn't sure what to make of Beth, but he definitely picked up on the familial resemblance. With red tones in their hair and bubbly personalities, the Meadows sisters were a matched set.

As promised, Beth slid into the seat beside him but waved Jameson over to sit across from her. She was talkative, and Haley was quieter than usual, letting her sister get to know everyone with her questions.

After breakfast, Camille pulled Asher to the side. "Hey. I noticed you didn't have a lot going on today. Would you mind helping us put up the tree in a little while?"

He'd let most of the bigger jobs pass him by today since he'd worked himself ragged yesterday, but he didn't mind helping out with the decorations. "Sure, just text me when you're ready for me."

"Great. It probably won't be until after lunch. We'll save the tree for last."

He tipped his hat at the women who were gathered around his mother getting instructions on where to find the Christmas decorations.

At lunchtime, Camille, Haley, and Beth had hung most of the garland and wreaths, as well as decorated the mantle and front porch, but they still weren't ready for the tree. Asher trudged back out into the cold day, hoping the weather would be more tolerable for the Christmas Parade after dark.

The sheet of gray clouds covering the sky foretold a different outcome.

It was three in the afternoon when Asher got Camille's text that they were ready for the tree. He made his way back to the house, but he didn't know what to think about Beth yet. She was friendly and bubbly, but he'd noticed how she turned every conversation at breakfast back to herself.

He reminded himself not to judge others, especially from one meeting. He grinned thinking about how his perception of Haley could've been irrevocably marred if they hadn't fixed things after that first meeting.

Beth was a guest at the ranch, like Haley, and they deserved his utmost kindness. He made it a point to give Beth another chance.

C amille dragged the pendant of her necklace along the gold chain as she studied the meeting room. "I think the tree should go in that corner. And that last bit of garland with the white lights above the entryway."

Haley dug into the hard plastic tote searching for the end of the garland. The plastic pine needles pricked her fingers. "Got it."

"Then a real wreath on the door. I'll make a note to get one next week. I think everyone would enjoy that. They smell so good."

Haley nodded. "I think so too. We have a lot of ribbon in here and could make some bows."

Camille waved a hand in the air. "I'll watch some YouTube videos tonight and figure it out. We can plan out where we intend to put them later."

Beth scrunched her nose. "I'm glad you know how to do all that creative stuff. It's not for me. Haley got all the creativity in the family."

"It's true." Haley gently kicked the large, rectangular box and asked, "You ready for the tree?"

"I think so," Camille said. "I texted Asher about five minutes ago. You think we can move it over there?"

"Sure. Let's all get on this side and push," Haley suggested.

Beth stepped back. "It's a little crowded. I'll just stay out of the way."

Camille and Haley crouched shoulder-to-shoulder on the same side of the box.

Haley counted. "One. Two. Three. Go."

They both shoved the box, using what little weight they had to get it to the other side of the room.

Haley grunted and let her hands slip down the cardboard. "How big is this tree?"

Camille panted and studied the high ceiling. "I don't know, but we might need a taller ladder."

"Let's see what we're working with." Haley cut

through the tape holding the box together and flipped open the lid. "That's a ton of branches."

Scratching her head, Camille studied the disassembled tree. "I guess that's why they have an artificial tree. A live tree this size would be too big and too heavy to get in here."

Beth chuckled. "It would only take a few of those strong cowboys. Wowza." She fanned her face dramatically.

Haley grinned. "The Hardings are nice to look at."

"Agreed," Camille said as she tugged a branch out of the box.

"I wish I could've seen Micah before he left," Beth said with a hand on her hip.

Haley hadn't mentioned to Beth that Micah had broken things off with her before he left. The only one she'd told was Gabby, and she hoped her sister hadn't spread the news. "Well, I guess we'd better get started. We only have a few hours until supper."

Asher showed up a few minutes later. "Put me to work, ladies."

Camille pointed to the box. "You put the branches on. We'll fluff."

They each dove into work, but the silence in the room was making Haley's skin crawl. After a few minutes, she couldn't take it any longer and began humming.

Asher stepped up behind her and asked, "Is that Randy Travis?"

Haley turned to him with a questioning "Hm?" He was only inches from her, and his dark eyes caught her attention.

"The song you were humming."

"Oh, yeah. It was 'Forever and Ever Amen.'"

"That's a good one."

Haley moved to fluff the next branch without looking up. Of course it was a good one. Bad songs didn't get stuck in people's heads.

When she took a break from humming, Camille picked up with "Fancy" by Reba McEntire. Haley guessed it immediately, but Camille kept the tune going for a while. When she fell quiet, Asher started his own tune. It was upbeat and catchy. Haley turned the tune over in her head, trying to piece it together with a song she'd heard before, but the answer was just out of reach.

When she snuck a glance at Asher, his expression was questioning. *Do you know the song?*

She didn't, and her inability to figure out the puzzle had her brows tugging together in confusion.

He grinned at her as he stuck the next branch in. When she shrugged, he belted out the first line of the chorus to 38 Special's "Caught up in You."

"That's not fair," Haley said. "I didn't know eighties rock was fair game."

"Welcome to my world," Beth said. "I never have a clue what you're humming."

Haley didn't pick up the humming game again because she didn't want Beth to feel left out. The next hour passed quickly, and the tree grew to its full height just as Lucas and Maddie arrived for supper.

Maddie looked up at the fluffy tree. "Wow. This looks amazing! I can't believe you did all of this."

Camille stepped off the ladder and wiped her brow with the back of her hand. "Me either. It was a chore. I couldn't have done it alone." She flashed a smile at Haley and Beth.

"I had fun. Maybe we can decorate the tree after supper," Haley suggested.

Camille closed up the empty tree box. "The Christmas Parade is tonight, remember?"

Haley cut a glance at the window and the darkness beyond. "Oh. I forgot about that."

Camille rested a hand on Haley's shoulder. "You can ride with Noah and me."

Haley tucked her chin as she redid her ponytail. "Um, I think I'll skip this one."

Beth slid to Asher's side. "Can I ride with you?"

Asher's gaze darted around the room before he said, "Sure."

Beth flashed a toothy smile. This morning, Beth had peppered Jameson and Asher with compliments and questions, but it seemed she'd settled on the Harding brother as her fling for the night.

Haley cleared her throat. "It sounds like fun, but I have some work I need to do tonight."

Asher narrowed his eyes at her as if her words confused him. She hadn't been discreet about her love of Christmas, and she wanted to hop in the truck and go to the Christmas Parade with everyone else. But while she'd told Asher about her fear of the dark, she hadn't told him the extent of her fear, and she didn't like to broadcast it if she could help it. It was embarrassing enough having to deal with it herself.

With the meeting room decked out for the holiday and the promise of a celebration to come, everyone beamed with excitement except Haley.

Nights like this, she hated the paralyzing fear that kept her from the things she loved most.

CHAPTER 13
ASHER

The ride into town was short, and Beth talked most of the way. Asher tried to listen, but her monologue jumped from friends to the elementary class she taught to skiing, and he found himself confused by all the names. She certainly had a lot of excitement for the things she talked about.

His thoughts drifted to Haley more than once on the drive. He'd seen sadness in her eyes when she announced she wasn't coming to the parade. It didn't add up. She'd made it clear that she loved Christmas, and suddenly she didn't want to go to the parade.

When Beth paused for a split second, Asher took the opportunity to get his own words in. "Why didn't Haley come tonight?"

Beth tilted her chin up and scanned the road ahead. They were coming into downtown Blackwater, and Christmas lights lit up the streets. "She doesn't go out at night."

"What?"

Beth turned to him. "She's scared of the dark."

Asher drew his brows together. He recalled her flippant comment about being afraid of the dark on the first day they'd gone out on the ranch. "So, she doesn't go outside at all after the sun goes down?"

"Never. She's been that way for a long time. She just panics and runs back inside."

He parked parallel to the sidewalk at the end of a long line of cars. "That sounds awful."

"Tell me about it. I don't think she went to a single football game in high school," Beth said.

He stepped out of the truck and walked around the front to open Beth's door. She happily accepted his helping hand when she slid out of the truck and then kept her hold on it.

He pulled his hand away as they moved into the downtown square. Beth walked closer to him as the crowd of people became denser. By the time they caught up with the rest of the ranch crew, she had wrapped both hands around his arm and had her shoulder pressed against his. He tried not to let on how embarrassed he was to have her pressed against his side while they waited for the parade to begin.

It wasn't often he found himself at a loss for words, but Beth had talked enough for both of them on the ride over. He caught sight of Sticky Sweets Bakery on the next block and asked, "You want some hot chocolate?"

Beth lifted one shoulder. "Sure."

When she released his hand, he took the freedom and ran. He didn't care if he had to wait in line for half an hour. He needed time to hear himself think.

Beth was fun, but she'd dominated the conversation. He much preferred the easy back-and-forth he experienced with Haley. Variety in conversation kept things exciting.

He stepped up next to Beth and handed her the warm cup as the first float crept along Main Street. Elves tossed candy to kids on the sidewalk while lights flashed around their feet. Beth waved in excitement as a float passed with young kids on it from the elementary school. She pointed out a few others that caught her attention.

"Here they come!" Camille shouted.

Everyone pushed up onto their toes to catch a glimpse of Lucas and Maddie dressed as Santa and Mrs. Claus. They waved with bright smiles as the float moved to the end of the street.

"He said he'd wait until the end," Camille said.

"Who?" Beth asked.

"Lucas is going to propose to Maddie on the float," Asher said.

Beth clasped her hands together. "Oh, that's so sweet!"

They all watched as Lucas knelt in front of Maddie, and the crowd went wild. Shouts and whistles echoed through the freezing night.

Asher clapped and whooped as the happy couple embraced, and he wished Haley could be here to see this. She'd want to celebrate with the family.

When the parade was over, Beth was shivering with her arms wrapped around her middle. "It's so cold. I can't feel my nose or my toes."

Asher looked down at her heeled boots. "We should get you back. We're expecting light snow tonight."

She didn't object as she followed him back to the truck. As soon as she settled into the passenger seat, she was turning knobs on the dash.

"Is this the heat?"

"Yeah, but it takes a minute to warm up." He patted the steering wheel. "Old truck."

She shivered most of the way back to the ranch, which kept her quiet. He didn't see the point in breaking the silence, and he didn't want to hum after Beth's remarks earlier.

As soon as he shifted the truck into park at the main house, Beth jumped out and jogged inside with her arms tucked close around herself. He tried to keep pace with her, but she was determined to get out of the cold.

She opened the door and tripped over the threshold. Asher quickly grabbed her upper arm, preventing her from falling to the hard wooden floor.

"Have a nice trip."

Asher looked up to see Haley sitting at the table with his guitar in her lap. She covered her mouth to hide the smile.

"See you next fall," Asher said, finishing the corny joke.

Haley threw her head back in laughter as Beth found her footing.

"I don't think it's very funny." Beth straightened her coat as pink tinted her cheeks.

"I'm sorry. I didn't mean to make fun of you," Asher said. He'd thought the joke was all in good fun, but if Beth couldn't laugh at herself then it wasn't a joke at all.

Haley stood and put the guitar on the table. "Oh, Beth. We weren't laughing at you. It's just a funny saying."

"If you say so. I'm ready for a hot bath. I may never thaw."

"I'll be up later," Haley said. "I still have some work to do. I've been goofing off too much tonight."

Beth pulled on the lapels of her coat. "See you in the morning."

Asher and Haley said a unified "Good night" as Beth walked up the stairs.

Haley gestured to the guitar. "I hope you don't mind, but I saw the guitar and assumed it was yours."

"You can play whenever you want. I'll leave it here so you can grab it when you feel like playing."

Her auburn hair was tied in a low ponytail that hung over her right shoulder, and she brushed her fingers along the soft waves. "Thanks, it's been a while since I've played."

"You're always welcome to mine." He stuck his hands in the front pockets of his jeans.

Being around Beth all night had been exhausting. He'd fought off her advances at every turn. With Haley, he could finally relax. "So, Lucas proposed to Maddie tonight on the float."

Haley's eyes grew wide. "You're kidding! That's awesome."

His own mouth tugged up on one side at her excitement. "I thought you'd like that. I'm sure Maddie will tell you all about it tomorrow."

Haley's shoulders sank. "I hate that I missed it."

Asher tucked his chin and scraped his boot against the floor. "Why didn't you come?"

She pursed her lips to one side. "It's embarrassing."

That confirmed Beth's words from earlier. "You don't have to tell me." He already knew, but he wished he didn't if she'd rather he not know.

Haley blurted, "I'm afraid of the dark." She grinned, but there wasn't any happiness in her eyes.

"I'm sorry." What else could he say?

She shrugged. "I really need to get some more work done tonight. I'll see you in the morning."

"Good night." He pushed the word through his tightening throat.

Asher felt an unfamiliar and unwelcome pain in his chest as he watched her walk away. He hated knowing she was afraid of something that kept her from experiencing some of the things she loved.

It was heartache. His heart broke with hers because he knew exactly how it felt when fear stood in the way of happiness.

CHAPTER 14
ASHER

Beth didn't try to sit by Asher at church the next morning, and he was equal parts relieved and remorseful. He was glad she'd moved on from whatever infatuation she'd had yesterday, but he was pretty sure he'd hurt her feelings with the tripping joke.

He shouldn't have said it, and he'd apologized, but it seemed Beth wasn't an easy forgiver. She was leaving after church, and it didn't sit well with him that they'd landed on bad terms.

After the service, he caught up to Beth just outside the church. "Hey, Beth."

She turned quickly, fanning her strawberry-blonde hair. "Hey."

"Can I offer you a ride back to the ranch?"

Her peppy smile was back. "I can't say no to

that, cowboy." She linked her arm around his elbow and slid in close as they walked to his truck.

When they were both settled in the truck, he spoke first. "What time are you leaving today?

"As soon as we get back."

"So, did you enjoy your trip this weekend?" He winced as soon as the words were out. "I mean, your vacation." How many times could he offend her with the tripping joke?

If Beth noticed, she didn't let it slow her down. "I did. The ranch living isn't really my thing, but it's good for a few days with Haley."

"So, the two of you are close?" He looked both ways before pulling out of the church parking lot.

"Of course. We have a brother that's the eldest. Then there's me, then our other brother, then Haley. By the time she came along, I was aching for a sister. Then more brothers and sisters came along, but Haley and I bonded before that. We're the two most outgoing of the Meadows family. Haley is always up for anything. I guess that's how she ended up here on a whim to meet Micah."

"Yeah. Too bad he hasn't been here all week. She came here to get to know him, and she got to know the rest of the family instead."

"That's not a bad thing," Beth said. "I don't know Micah, but you and Haley are like two peas in a pod."

Asher tightened his grip on the steering wheel. "What makes you think that?"

"Well, you both have that quirky sense of humor that I don't understand." Beth twirled her finger in the air. "And she talked about you a little last night."

He kept his eyes on the road, refusing to react to her words.

"She said you write songs. I know you don't know how much that means to her, but it's something she's really passionate about. She's been making up songs since we were kids, and she's good at it. I think she understands music better than she understands people."

Asher knew what it was like to live with a song in his head, and knowing Haley was just like him in yet another way had his heart pounding.

Beth shifted in her seat. "It's too bad she didn't meet you first."

His jaw tensed until his teeth ached. He had met Haley first, but that didn't change things. She'd talked to his brother first, and it made all the difference in his mind.

"Haley is great. I like hanging out with her, but we're just friends."

Beth shrugged. "Okay. If you say so. I teach kids for a living. Physical reactions speak louder than words, and you're too tense right now to be telling the truth."

Asher's eyes grew wide as his attention whipped to Beth.

She held up her hands. "Don't worry. I won't tell. I knew last night. You were uncomfortable around me at the parade, but when we got back to the ranch and Haley was there, you changed."

He turned his attention back to the road as they turned into the drive leading to the ranch. "Please don't say anything."

"I would never do that," Beth said.

Asher bit the inside of his cheek. If Beth had picked up on his feelings for Haley, who else could tell?

He parked in front of the main house, and Beth placed a hand on his arm. "Relax. Everything will work out."

Asher swallowed and nodded.

"Thanks for the ride." She pulled her hand away, and her smile had lost all hint of flirtation.

"Have a safe trip home." Asher sighed and hung his head. He had to stop bringing up the trip joke.

Beth narrowed her eyes. "Very funny, wise guy."

He grinned. "I'm sorry about the joke last night. I wasn't trying to make fun of you for tripping."

"Oh, I know." She waved her hand. "I'm used to Haley's humor. She's one of those that can laugh at herself, so I get it."

"It was great meeting you," Asher said.

"Bye." She stepped out of his truck just as Camille and Haley were pulling in.

Asher went inside and helped his parents get lunch ready. Beth's words pinged around in his head like the ball in a pinball machine, but he tried to push them from his mind. He'd call Micah this evening to get an update on the bull. He could be on his way back right now. With Micah here, Haley would be spending her time with him, and Asher wouldn't have to worry about any misplaced feelings for her. She was dating his brother, and that was the end of it.

Asher was playing thumb war with Levi after lunch while Aaron helped with the meal cleanup. Levi was competitive, and Asher was getting a wrist cramp.

"Boys, what are your plans for the day?" Mama Harding asked.

"I'm free. Levi can hang out with me today," Asher said.

"Actually, I wanted to see if you'd take Haley to the rivers. She needs a few more photos, and the website will be finished."

Another day spent with Haley sounded like bliss and torture knotted into a conflicting bow, but if Mama said it, that meant it was already set in stone. "Sure, Levi can come with us."

"He's coming with me to the store," Mama Harding said. "We're making cookies."

Levi threw his hands up. "Yes! Cookies!"

Haley stepped off the stairs and raised her camera to her face, then immediately lowered it and pressed a few buttons. "You ready?"

Asher nodded, unsure if he could trust his voice.

Her energetic smile spread wide. "Cowboy up."

Asher followed her to his truck on autopilot. Her hair was piled in a bun, and a thin scarf was tied around her head. He shifted his attention to the floor instead of the exposed skin of her neck.

She turned on the radio as soon as he started the engine. She scanned through five songs before leaving it on an old country tune.

"So, tell me a little bit about where we're going. Don't skimp on the details. I need pretty words for the website."

He narrowed his eyes as he studied the trail leading to Bluestone Creek. "Idyllic setting nestled at the foothills of the Big Horn Mountains."

"Keep talking."

"There might not be much to see this time of year except snow."

Haley shrugged. "The snow will make a pretty picture too. I'll come back a few times to grab some photos in the other seasons to update."

Asher rested his wrist on the steering wheel. "You're coming back?"

She lifted one eyebrow. "Have you seen this place? I may never leave."

A pain shot through his chest. What would it be like if Haley stayed? Having her around was amazing and torturous at the same time.

At the top of the next low rise, Haley scooted to the edge of her seat. "Stop. Right here."

Haley was opening the door of the truck before it had come to a complete stop. She stood on the running board and took a few photos before climbing back in and checking them. "Good. Next."

They stopped once more before the creek came into view. When she spotted the snow-covered banks, her gaze swept back and forth over the scene. "This is perfect."

Asher parked well away from the bank to make sure the tire tracks didn't show up in her photos, and they both got out. The wind gusted from time to time, but Haley didn't let the cold interfere. She lifted the camera, lowered it, stepped to a new spot, and repeated.

Five minutes later, she made her way back to the truck where Asher waited.

"Is there another spot where I can see the creek?"

"Sure. I know of a good place where this one intersects Blackwater."

"Another creek?" she asked as she climbed into the truck.

"Blackwater River."

"Oh, I definitely need photos of the namesake."

She kept her head down during the majority of the drive but peeked up from time to time to make sure she wasn't missing another photo opportunity.

When she saw the next river come into view, she reached out to touch his arm. "Right here."

They were still fifty yards from the creek, but he stopped and killed the engine. He hung back by the truck and watched as the wheels in her head turned, evaluating all angles and possibilities of the scenery.

A few minutes later, she came back to the truck. "Can I get on the roof again?"

Asher linked his hands and offered them as a step onto the hood of the truck. She held tight to her camera with one hand and stepped up onto the hood, and then the roof.

"The sky is gorgeous today." She didn't look up from her camera.

"You should see the sunset," Asher remarked.

She took a deep breath, and a thick fog formed in front of her face as she released the warm air. "I'd love to. I'm usually getting ready to settle in for the night by sunset."

They still had plenty of hours until sunset, but the urgency in her statement had him calculating the remaining hours of the day.

"I think I have what I need." She crouched to

crawl down onto the hood before reaching out to him.

Asher helped her down and released her the moment her feet touched the ground. He blamed the cold and his body's urgent desire for warmth for the urge he felt to pull her in close.

They parted at the front of the truck to go their separate ways. When the doors had closed them into the truck, he turned the key. The engine sputtered without firing, and he tried again. The starter didn't catch. He concealed his worry and tried once more.

"Is it going to start?" she asked.

Asher pulled his lips into a thin line. "I don't think so."

"Do you know what's wrong?"

"Not yet. Let me check a few things. It's an old truck, so there are a dozen possibilities."

He grabbed his hat and stepped out into the cold. Under the hood, he checked the few things he knew he could assess and fix on his own. None of them were the culprit, so he closed the hood and got back in.

"You fix it?" she asked. Thankfully, her tone didn't hold a reprimand.

"Nope. I know a little about mechanics, but not enough. Micah is the one who tinkers around here."

"And he's gone. Yikes."

Asher found his phone and made a call. "First phone-a-friend is Lucas."

A few rings later, Asher got the voicemail and moved on to Noah who answered on the second ring.

"Hello."

"Hey, Haley and I are stuck out at the river. Can you come pick us up? My truck needs some help."

"Sure. I'll bring the toolbox. Give me about ten minutes to get there."

Asher disconnected the call. "He's coming."

"Well, at least we don't have to sit out in the cold," Haley said.

"Ever the optimist. I'm sorry about this."

She shrugged. "It's fine. Things happen."

"You want to get some more photos while we're here?"

She shook her head. "I'd rather stay in the warm."

"I get it." He leaned onto the steering wheel. "The clouds are showing out today." Fluffy whites spread over most of the sky against a vibrant blue background.

"I know. I love clouds. I used to lie in the yard with my brother, Connor, and point out shapes we found."

Asher narrowed his eyes at the clouds. "Like what?"

She pointed at a cloud. "That one looks like a dragon."

He tilted his head, willing a dragon to reveal itself. "I don't see it."

She moved her finger in the air. "That's the nose, there's the tail, and it has short arms in the front."

"I've got nothing."

Haley chuckled. "It's because your imagination is audible, not optical."

"Come again?"

"You write songs and identify with music. You can create new tunes and words out of nothing. It's like painting and drawing, but you use your sight to help bring the colors and images together to make something new to look at. It's the same concept, just fueled by different senses."

"Wow. I hadn't thought about it that way. So you have both?"

She turned her attention back to the clouds. "I guess so. They do have one thing in common."

"What's that?" he asked.

"They're pieced together with the emotions we feel. Auditory and visual art often imitate life."

"You're saying we put our feelings in songs?"

She grinned. "That's exactly what I'm saying."

Asher took a deep breath and studied the clouds again, searching for something only she could see. "It's harder than it looks."

"Don't force it. Just let your mind shift the outline of the clouds into something recognizable."

"Okay, this is definitely harder than it looks."

She chuckled. "Don't hurt yourself, cowboy. It's not a test."

"I know."

"Can I hear one of your songs?" she asked.

He turned his attention to her. "Sure. I don't keep them a secret. I usually play a few originals at Barn Sour."

Her words became soft and uncertain. "But I'd have to go out after dark to be there."

Could she really go her whole adult life without going out after dark? The severity of her fear was hard for him to fathom. "I can play after dinner one night. I wouldn't make you go out if you didn't want to." He wanted to share that part of himself with her, but asking her to face the discomfort of her fear wasn't something he was willing to do.

"Thanks," she whispered.

Asher leaned his forehead against the steering wheel and closed his eyes. He wasn't supposed to feel drawn to a woman who was interested in his brother. It went against everything he believed in. He'd gladly put his family above himself any day. Even today, when he wanted to reach for her hand more than he wanted his next breath.

Had she been talking to Micah while he was gone? Asher hadn't heard from his brother once in the last week. Was Micah eager to get back to the ranch to get to know Haley? Asher knew his brother was missing out, and it felt as if he were stealing this time with Haley from Micah.

Silence filled the cab, and Asher's thoughts spiraled into guilt. "Have you heard from Micah?"

Haley shook her head but didn't say anything. They both turned when they heard the rumble of a truck.

She wrapped her arms around her middle. "That must be Noah, here to save the day."

"Our hero drives a Ford," Asher joked.

Haley chuckled and jumped out of the truck. When they filed into Noah's truck, Haley scooted into the middle, and Asher took his place beside her on the bench seat.

Being forced to sit so close to her in the smaller truck had his mind tugging in different directions. Cling to the door, or let his shoulder rest against hers?

Haley didn't seem to be bothered by the close proximity as she chatted with Noah about the photos she'd taken and her intentions for the website.

Asher leaned back against the headrest and closed his eyes. *You don't like Haley. She's just a friend. You don't remember kissing her. She's just a friend.*

Maybe if he repeated the words, they would become true.

CHAPTER 15
HALEY

Haley held out an apple treat to Weston. "You like those?"

Maddie huffed a laugh. "That one has a sweet tooth. He'll pester you for treats."

Haley rubbed his mane. "I don't blame you. I like sweet treats too."

She'd spent the morning photographing the Christmas decorations in the meeting room and caught a ride to the stable with Maddie after lunch. Hanging out with Maddie and the horses was much better than sitting in her room alone.

"Dolly could use a few, too, if you want to give them to her. She likes the ones in the red package."

Haley jumped at the chance to spoil the horse and grabbed two treats.

The door creaked at the other end of the stables, and Asher walked in. With his thick coat and hat down low, he could've passed for any of the Harding men, but Haley recognized the tentative walk and long stride. It was definitely Asher.

As he approached, he removed his hat and tousled his hair. "Everything go okay today?"

Maddie patted Haley's shoulder. "I wouldn't say she's a natural, but we're working on it."

Haley faced Asher and crossed her arms. "Did you come to check on me?" she asked playfully.

Asher's gaze bounced around the room, and he shoved his hands into his coat pockets. "Something like that. You ready to go? I'll give you a ride to supper."

Haley looked back to Maddie. "See you in a few."

Maddie waved her hand. "I'll be there shortly."

Asher jerked his head toward the door, and Haley followed him, slipping on her gloves and wrapping her coat tighter around her body in anticipation of the cold.

When Asher opened the door, he stood to the side for her to go first, but she stopped in the doorway, halted by the inky darkness that covered everything in sight.

"It's dark." She hadn't kept track of the time, and the sun had completely set. There wasn't even a moon out to temper the black void.

Asher stepped in front of her but averted his gaze. His voice was merely a whisper. "I didn't know how serious you were when you said you were afraid of the dark."

Haley nodded emphatically. "Very serious," she whispered back. She looked behind her into the dimly lit stable and swallowed hard.

Asher moved closer, and the shadow from his hat was so dark she couldn't see his eyes. "Are you okay?"

She shook her head and backed up a step.

He caught her gloved hand in his, gripping tight. "You can't stay in the stables all night. Tell me how to help you."

Her panic was growing, and she couldn't hear anything over the roaring in her ears.

Asher lifted her chin with his other hand. "Haley. Focus on me. How can I help?"

Tears were flooding her eyes, and she knew they would roll down her face if she spoke. Why did she have to be afraid of something as mundane as the dark? Everyone else could go about their lives after the sun went down, but it had been years since Haley had made the mistake of losing track of time.

Asher sucked in a deep breath. "Breathe with me."

She followed his lead and tightened her grip on his hand. She needed the light of morning like she needed air, and her lungs were screaming.

"Now, let's try something. Repeat after me," Asher whispered.

Haley nodded.

Asher leaned in close, vying for her attention against the darkness. "When I am afraid, I put my trust in You."

Haley repeated, "When I am afraid, I put my trust in you."

"Say it again."

"When I am afraid, I put my trust in you."

Asher took her other hand in his and took a step back, tugging her with him. "Now, keep saying it, and let me lead you."

Haley chanted the words, and she trembled as she took the first step. Her heart was beating wildly, and the words began to break.

No, she needed the words, and she willed herself to focus on repeating them perfectly.

Asher turned to open the truck door and laid a hand on her back to lead her in. The dim cab light was enough to settle her shaking, but she was keenly aware of the darkness on every side of the truck. She rested her hands on the dash, desperate for an anchor.

Asher jumped into the driver's seat and started the engine of Hunter's truck. "Not much longer. You're doing great."

Haley kept her head down. "I bet you didn't expect this when you showed up this evening." When Asher didn't respond, she turned to look at him.

His face was grave, gaze locked on the road ahead.

"Thank you. For understanding. And helping."

He rubbed a hand over her back. "I wish I was better at this."

She tucked her chin and focused on breathing. Her stomach was beginning to roll, and she slowly released a breath through her mouth.

A minute later, as promised, Asher shifted the truck into park in front of the main house.

He opened his door an inch to keep the cab light on and turned to her. "Listen, we're the first ones here, so when we get inside, you can sneak up to your room and calm down. Do you need me to come with you?"

Haley shook her head. "I'll be okay when I get inside."

"I'll come around and get you." Asher jumped out of the truck and opened the door on her side within seconds. He took her hands in his and squeezed. "Hey, remember what to say."

"When I am afraid, I will trust in you," Haley recited.

"You know I don't mean me, right?" he asked.

Haley furrowed her brow and looked up. She needed something to focus on—an anchor—and her gaze fell on his eyes, staring back at her.

"What?" she whispered.

"It's a Psalm. When I am afraid, I put my trust in You."

Haley nodded. "Right. Okay." She didn't understand at all, but now wasn't the time to figure it out.

She focused on Asher's eyes as he led her out of the truck.

"Say it," he reminded her.

"When I am afraid, I put my trust in you." She said the words at least five more times before they reached the steps at the porch. She couldn't look down.

Asher guided her. "Step up." Then another. "Step up."

She followed his commands until they reached the door. He released one of her hands to open it, letting out the light, and she could breathe again. Stepping into the bright house felt like breaking the surface of the water after straining to breathe. Her lungs ached, and she wanted to cry in relief.

When she was safely inside the door, Asher released her other hand and broke his stare.

She wanted to say something—anything—but her petty thanks weren't enough. He'd led her through the dark and anchored her through the terrifying triumph over her fears.

"Thank you." The words were soft and broken.

He was her anchor.

He rubbed his jaw and stared at the floor. "You're welcome."

Haley bit her lips between her teeth and stepped around him. She wanted to hug him and release the tears that were begging to be set free, but he might not want that. She wasn't supposed to want that, and the realization stabbed in her chest.

Appreciation and longing tugged her toward him, and she resented Gabby's advice to let the Lord do His work in her life. She wanted to run headlong for what she wanted—*who* she wanted.

A spark of truth grew into a flame within her. She wanted Asher's arms around her, and she wanted to believe that the longing in his eyes meant he wanted the same.

She turned and headed for the stairs leading to her room.

She'd gotten lost in his eyes, but it felt like home.

CHAPTER 16
HALEY

Haley crept down the stairs only minutes before Mama Harding signaled everyone to line up for supper. It had taken longer than Haley had expected to calm down once she'd shut herself in her room. The familiar fear mixed with her conflicted reactions to Asher's presence had her thoughts twisting and knotting into a jumbled mess.

She spotted him in the crowded room and forced a grin. She'd become a master at avoiding the dark over the years, but she'd given Asher a front-row seat to her ridiculous fear early on. It wasn't the first time her nyctophobia had put her in an embarrassing situation.

Haley assumed her place at the beginning of the line, but Asher squeezed himself in next to her.

"Let's move it, small fry. I'm starving."

Haley grabbed the tongs in front of her. "You skipped lunch. What did you expect?"

"I expected to pay for my mistake, but a long workday on just biscuits and sausage is rough," Asher said. He tapped his foot to a familiar beat as he hummed the tune.

Haley whispered without looking up, "'The Devil Went Down to Georgia.'"

"Lucky guess," Asher said. "Maybe it's the only country song with a beat that fast."

Haley pulled her lips to one side. "John Michael Montgomery has a fast one. Something about an auction."

Asher snapped his fingers. "'Sold.'"

"Yes! I love that one."

Asher began humming the upbeat tune and bobbing his head to the fast-paced chorus.

She'd have to thank him again for not only saving her from the darkness, but driving out her lingering embarrassment.

At the table, Noah led the prayer, and Camille shooed everyone down the bench seat so she could squeeze in beside Haley. "So, how did it go with the horses today?"

"It was amazing!" Haley squealed. "Somehow, I'm exhausted, but I don't think we did anything physically demanding today."

Lucas stabbed a bite of meat with his fork. "It's

freezing outside, and your body is constantly working to stay warm."

"True story," Aaron said. "Levi hasn't refused a nap since the first frost."

Haley nudged Levi's shoulder. "What did you do today?"

"I helped Dad feed the cows. Then we checked the fences. Then we mixed the feed for tomorrow. Then we gave Biscuit a bottle!"

"Biscuit?"

"That's the bottle calf. Her mommy didn't feed her like she was supposed to."

Haley rested a hand on her chest. "Oh no."

"It's okay. We feed her," Levi said.

"So, you just hold out the bottle, and she drinks it?" Haley asked.

Levi shook his head. "No, Daddy has to stand with his legs on both sides of her and hold her still. She gets scared because she doesn't know we're helping her." He waved his hands in the air as he explained.

"You sound like you know what you're doing."

Levi lifted his chin. "I do. I work on the ranch a lot."

Haley snuck a glance at Aaron who wore a satisfied grin. The littlest Harding was growing into a rancher at an early age.

Haley ate while Levi told her how they bale hay

in the summer. He shoved a few hasty bites into his mouth whenever she asked questions.

After dinner, Haley helped Mama Harding clean up while everyone else talked about the day and what tomorrow would hold for each of them.

The workers were still scattering when the supper mess was cleaned up, and Haley waved a lazy good-bye to the few remaining.

In her room, she sent the photos she'd taken today to her laptop and chose the ones she would edit. She'd gotten a little carried away today, but the horses were so beautiful. She had plenty to work with for the website.

Her lap desk still hadn't arrived, and sitting on the bed with her back against the headboard wasn't cutting it. So much for expedited shipping. She threw off the blankets, changed into a thick sweater and sweatpants, and grabbed her laptop. The meeting room would be empty, and she could work without killing her back.

She slunk down the stairs in her socked feet, careful to keep a tight grip on her laptop. Halfway down the stairs, she heard music. The start and stop of the thrum of a guitar made her pause. She didn't want to intrude, but her curiosity was pushing her forward. The tune was good for the brief seconds it existed, and then tentative and unsure before ending abruptly.

Peeking into the meeting room, she spotted

Asher sitting atop a stool on the far side of the long room. His head was bowed, bobbing to a silent rhythm before his fingers slid over the strings.

Haley tiptoed to the table and gently set her laptop on the worn surface before turning to run back up the stairs. In her room, she grabbed her camera, a sketchpad, and a pencil.

Asher still hadn't looked up from his instrument when she returned, and she moved closer to him with her camera ready. When he looked up, she shrugged one shoulder and lifted her camera.

His nod was almost imperceptible, but it was the permission she needed. Moving in a semi-circle around him, she captured his thoughtful process. His hair was wildly sticking up in all directions, and a grease stain marred his left cheek, but the image was beautiful—unfiltered and emotional.

When she settled directly in front of him, ready to capture his likeness, a flicker of recognition made her pause.

She lowered the camera when the answer came to her—the man in her dream. He'd been a faceless figure then, but she had the strangest feeling she was seeing the completed image.

Shaken by the recognition, she walked back to the table to trade her camera for the sketchpad. She flipped through the pages until she found the one she'd sketched on the day she'd arrived at Blackwater Ranch.

It looked just as she remembered. It looked like Asher.

She turned to where he played, struck by the realization. The lines of his jaw and the curves of his shoulders were identical to the sketch.

Asher lifted his chin and continued to play the soothing tune. She laid the sketch pad on the table and stepped toward him. She moved closer with each chord he played, called home by an invisible magnet.

His gaze didn't leave hers, and when she stood close enough to reach out and touch him, he spoke.

"Do you want to play one of your songs?"

She did. She wanted to feel the vibrations of the music and create beautiful sounds more than anything.

But instead of being honest, she shook her head.

Asher's mouth tugged to one side, revealing a handsome grin. "Liar."

She didn't deny it.

"Why won't you play?" he asked.

She didn't answer. The only thing keeping her from reaching for the guitar was fear.

When I am afraid, I put my trust in you.

The verse Asher taught her rang in her mind, and she found the courage to accept the invitation.

Asher stood and let her have the stool, but he stayed close, arms crossed over his chest.

The guitar was familiar and new at the same

time, but she welcomed the adjustment. She took her time warming up before playing her favorite song all the way through. She didn't add the lyrics, but it felt freeing to play the song for another person. It was the first time she'd shared it beyond her bedroom walls.

When she finished, she handed the guitar back to Asher without making eye contact. She moved to brush past him, fighting the embarrassment of exposing herself to criticism.

Asher wrapped his hand around her arm. "Wait."

She turned to him, but the only thing she found in his eyes was exhaustion. She stood there, waiting for him to speak and wishing he wouldn't.

Asher cleared his throat and whispered, "Why are you afraid of the dark?"

Haley released the tense breath she'd been holding and relaxed. She could hear his concern, and it softened her heart.

"Because my sister locked me in the basement when I was five years old."

Asher's expression didn't change, but she felt his grip tighten on her arm and knew he'd tensed every muscle in his body.

"It was an accident," she clarified, "but I was alone in the dark for an hour before my parents realized I was missing."

"I'm sorry." His words were coated in comfort.

"I don't want to remember, but I do. I was terrified and screaming the whole time, and I couldn't find my way." She swallowed the lump in her throat and felt the tingling in her nose that meant her tears were close. "Every time I'm in the dark, I feel like that kid in the basement again."

Asher wrapped his arms around her, and she rested her head on his shoulder. Every breath brought her closer to exhaustion as she relaxed in his arms.

"I'm sorry," he whispered against her hair.

"Thank you for helping me tonight." She could fall asleep right here, safe in his arms.

He released her and nodded. "Anytime."

She pointed her thumb over her shoulder. "I need to get to bed, and you look like you're about to turn into a pumpkin."

He rubbed a hand over his face and scratched the top of his head. "I'm exhausted."

"Why were you playing instead of sleeping?" she asked.

"I'm playing at Barn Sour this weekend, and I needed to run through the set."

Haley brushed a hand over her head and down her ponytail. "It sounds great."

"Thanks. And thank you for letting me hear your song. When can I hear the lyrics?" he asked.

She shrugged. "When I write them." She lazily waved. "Good night."

"Good night."

She gathered up her laptop, sketchpad, and camera before trudging up the stairs. Locked in the quiet space of her room, she laid her things on the dresser and slipped into the bed. She left the light on and hoped it would be enough to keep the nightmares at bay.

Squeezing her eyes closed, she sucked in a lungful of air and began praying.

Her eyes snapped open. The verse.

Tossing the blankets off, she knelt in front of her suitcase and dug around until she found her Bible. Asher said it was a Psalm, but which one?

She crawled to the nightstand and grabbed her phone. A quick Google search of the words gave her the answer, and she crawled back to her Bible. She flipped the pages to chapter fifty-six and slid her finger down the page until she found the third verse.

"When I am afraid, I put my trust in You."

She leaned back against the bed. Asher wanted her to give her fears to the Lord, but could she release the stifling hold it had on her?

Rubbing her finger over the word in question, she knew she had to try.

You.

Maybe she didn't need an anchor. Maybe she needed faith.

CHAPTER 17
HALEY

The next day, she was able to hang out at the main house with Levi. Spending time with the kid was relaxing and fun, as well as a nice break from work. He had a handful of board games he loved, and when they'd played through them, he brought her a box filled with his rock collection. She listened as he poured over the story behind each one —where he'd found them and when, along with a name.

After lunch, Levi went out on the ranch with his dad, and Haley was able to get some work out of the way. Her business was booming so close to Christmas, and she didn't resent the extra work. It kept her mind busy and free from dangerous thoughts about the brown-eyed cowboy who made beautiful music and invaded her dreams.

Camille was the first to arrive for supper shortly

after Haley had come downstairs to help Mama Harding finish up the cooking.

"Hey, need a hand?" Camille asked.

"I think we're ready," Haley said as she eyed Camille's sweater dress. "You look cute!"

"Thanks. We're going to Barn Sour tonight. You in?"

"It's Tuesday night."

"Is it a school night?" Camille taunted. "We don't have to wait for the weekend to live a little."

"I can't argue with that." Even as she said the words, anxiety pressed against the walls of her chest. What excuse could she give for not joining them tonight?

Asher stepped up beside Haley as she finished speaking. She hadn't even noticed him come in.

"She already said she would ride with me," Asher said. "We're going to head on over early so she can help me set up the equipment. Hunter usually does it, but since he isn't here, I asked Haley."

Camille's eyes widened. "Oh, that's a great idea. I didn't even think of it. Okay, we'll catch up with you later."

The plan to set up together was news to Haley too. He hadn't asked her. Had he meant to and forgotten? Better yet, had he forgotten her irrational fear of the dark?

When Camille walked off to greet Noah, Asher leaned in to whisper to Haley.

"If you don't want to go, that's okay, but I thought we might be able to go early and give you time to get settled before everyone else gets there."

The thought of stepping out into the dark again had her nerves dancing, but the opportunity to hear Asher play and sing for a crowd was something she didn't want to miss. "Let me change out of my work clothes."

"Sure. I'll wait here."

Haley ran up the stairs and threw on a brown sweater and dark-wash jeans with her rust-colored booties. She shook her hair out of the ponytail and grabbed her small purse from the top of the dresser. She was ready, but she didn't want to leave just yet. She'd have to face her fear soon if she wanted the chance to hear Asher play. Closing her eyes, she took deep breaths and said a silent prayer for peace and strength. When she'd dawdled enough, she crept back down to the meeting room.

Asher stood leaning over the table, propped on his hands, listening to Lucas. She made her way to Asher's side, and his bright smile appeared when he noticed her.

"Ready to go?" he asked.

"As ready as I'll ever be," she grumbled.

They waved their good-byes as Asher followed her to the door. He flipped on the porch lights, and when she stepped outside, she squinted against the bright headlights pointed her way.

Asher grabbed her hand, capturing her attention. "Does the light help?"

Haley nodded. "It does a little. Let's get this over with."

"You remember what to do?"

Haley nodded. "Run for the truck."

Asher chuckled, and the joyful sound eased her discomfort.

"I mean the verse. Did it help last time?"

It had helped, and she planned to do more than just chant the words this time. If Asher would lead her, she could close her eyes and pray the words. "It did. I'm ready."

Haley closed her eyes as Asher took her other hand in his. He led her across the porch, down the steps, and to his truck. When he opened the door, his hand moved to her back to guide her inside. Once she was settled, he closed the door, and the cab lights went out in the truck he'd borrowed from Hunter.

Panic began to build in her until Asher opened the driver's side door and the lights came back on. He punched a button on the ceiling of the truck, and the lights stayed.

"Just hang tight. We'll be there before you know it." Asher started the truck and shifted into reverse.

The ride to Barn Sour could have lasted minutes or hours. The time lost its meaning as she repeated the prayer Asher had taught her. The words sounded funny in her head after about the twentieth time she said them, and she focused on the last word—You.

When the smooth ride of the road turned to gravel beneath the tires, Asher patted her shoulder. "Almost there." He put the truck in park and killed the engine. "Let's get you inside."

Asher led her inside, and the corners of her lips began to turn up by the time he ushered her into Barn Sour.

"Haley?"

His tentative voice encouraged her to open her eyes. The place had a rustic vibe with weathered wooden walls, vintage plaques, and neon signs. She didn't know where to look first.

"Wow. This is so cool."

"That's what you have to say?" Asher said as he crossed his arms over his chest. "I feel like we just led an elephant through the eye of a sewing needle, and you're more interested in the atmosphere."

Haley threw her arms around Asher's neck and whispered into his neck, "Thank you. I can't believe I'm here."

His arms wrapped around her back, and his hand moved in comforting circles. "I'm proud of you."

She closed her eyes and said a quick prayer of thanks. "I haven't even been to a night service at church before. This is huge."

He leaned back to look at her, and she wanted

him to see the truth in her eyes. He'd stepped up and made it his mission to stand beside her as she faced her fear, and gratefulness filled her up.

Looking into his eyes, she knew she had to acknowledge the shift that had taken place tonight. Everything had changed between them—at least for her. It was as if she'd woken up from a lifetime of sleep, and nothing would ever be the same.

CHAPTER 18
ASHER

Asher guided Haley through the equipment setup as the other Hardings began arriving, and he was thankful that they'd each checked in with Haley to gauge her excitement for her first Barn Sour experience. The whole family hung out at what they called the Barn multiple times a week. The casual atmosphere provided the perfect opportunity to unwind after a back-breaking day at the ranch.

Asher and Haley were almost finished setting up when Donna, the restaurant owner, strode up to the stage with a friendly smile on her face. She was pushing sixty, but Donna had always been a life-of-the-party type. Her welcoming personality was one of the reasons the Barn was packed with locals every night.

"Hey, sweet cheeks. Who's your friend?" She

stuck a hand on her hip as she propped her shoulder against the wall.

One of Asher's eyebrows lifted in confusion before he scanned the restaurant. "Who?"

Donna dramatically gestured to Haley working beside him.

Oh, his *friend*. He would do well to remember Haley was just a friend. Maybe that was the trick to dispelling the nagging guilt he felt every time he enjoyed her company. He made a mental note to think *friends* every time he felt the urge to pull her in close.

He rested his guitar against the wall. "Donna, this is Haley—"

"Meadows. Nice to meet you." Haley extended her hand to the owner with a smile.

"It's a pleasure to have you tonight. Are you a singer too?"

"I am," Haley said.

"Are you singing with Asher this evening?"

Haley's eyes widened. "Oh, no. I'm just helping set up."

Asher jumped on the suggestion. "You can if you want to. Maybe this weekend? We'll have plenty of time to practice."

He waited impatiently for her answer, praying she'd agree. Hunter wouldn't mind letting her take his place for a night, and Asher was itching to hear her play and sing.

Haley rubbed a hand up and down her arm. "I don't know. Let me think about it."

That was as good as a yes. Her eyes were lit up in excitement.

Donna clapped her hand on her hip. "Well, just let me know when you decide. I can put your name on the flyers."

Haley didn't try to hide her excitement. "Thanks for the opportunity."

"Anytime. Any friend of Asher's is a friend of mine," Donna said.

With a wink and a knowing smile, Donna disappeared into the back room behind the bar.

Haley grabbed his arm. "Did you hear that? She invited me to sing!"

Asher fought to control his breathing. The elation on Haley's face had literally stolen his breath. He'd always thought that was a figure of speech.

Haley continued. "She hasn't even heard me sing before. Do you think she was just being polite?"

"No." Asher cleared his throat. "I think she was serious."

Haley bounced on her toes. "This is awesome. I'm going to tell Camille and Maddie."

Asher watched Haley make her way through the room and lean over a table surrounded by his family. They each congratulated her with hugs and friendly shoulder shoves.

He focused his attention on placing the wires where he wanted them. He could be friends with Haley. Everyone else in the family was doing a good job of being around her every day without crossing the line. He would just be her friend.

He cared about her like a friend. He hoped she was happy like he did all his other friends. Camille and Maddie had been around for a while, but even before they'd been in relationships with his brothers, he hadn't felt any romantic pull toward them. What was different about Haley?

Friends. He could be friends with the woman who showed up on their doorstep looking for Micah. It would probably help him solidify the friends label in his mind if he kept her connection to his brother front and center in his thoughts.

His time on the stage seemed to fly, but he'd spent the majority of the evening watching Haley laugh and attempt to dance with Camille and Maddie. Aaron tried to dance with her once, but she'd tripped over his boot and landed on the floor with a thud. Thankfully, she laughed at herself as Aaron helped her up and passed her off to Levi for a dance.

The ranch crew left in sets of two as the night wore on. Aaron and Levi were the first to go, followed by Lucas and Maddie, then Noah and Camille. By the last song of the night, Haley sat alone at a table on the far side of the room, finishing up a burger.

When he'd played his last chord, Haley lazily made her way to the stage and sat on the edge of the platform, tucking one foot under her. The night crowd was beginning to liven up, but thankfully, he was always gone before the mass of drinkers turned rowdy.

"You ready to pack up?" Haley asked. She blinked slowly as her shoulders sank.

Asher focused on rounding up the equipment so they could get home. "I can get it. We'll be out of here soon."

Haley stood and took her place beside him, silently tearing down everything they'd built earlier in the night. Later, she chatted with Donna while he loaded the equipment into the truck, and the two spitfire women seemed to hit it off. He joined them when everything was loaded and ready.

Donna wrapped an arm around Haley's shoulder and tugged her in close. "Where have you been hiding this one? She's a riot."

Asher shrugged. "She's something, isn't she?"

The tiredness she'd carried earlier was gone, replaced by an embarrassed blush and a smile. "Oh, stop it, you two. Donna, I had the best time tonight. I'll definitely be back, and if Asher will teach me a thing or two, I'd love to perform this weekend."

"You don't have to tell me twice," Donna said.

"I'll even send out a Tweet about it. People like me on Twitter."

Haley laughed. "I think people just love you in general."

"You said it." Donna melted back into the sea of tables and customers.

Haley grabbed his arm and squeezed. "We're going to be famous!"

Asher felt her joy filling his chest. "I don't know about you, but I'm already famous."

She slapped his chest. "This is fun. I can't believe it."

Asher scratched his brow. "I don't mean to end the fun, but are you ready to go?"

Haley's smile only faltered for a moment before determination lifted her shoulders. "I'm ready."

He patted her shoulder. "That's my girl."

Oops. Shoulder pat, yes. Claiming endearment, no. It was going to take him a while to cement her in the friend zone.

Haley squeezed the strap on her purse as she followed Asher to the door. He turned and waited for her quick nod before grabbing her hand and stepping into the darkness. Thankfully, Barn Sour had ample lighting in the parking lot, and he'd moved his truck to an open space near the entrance.

Within seconds, they were locked in the truck and cruising down the dark streets of Blackwater. Asher had to ease up on the accelerator a few times when his lead foot got the best of him. He had an uncontrollable urge to get her back to the ranch as quickly as possible. Watching her white-knuckled fists was making him uneasy.

When he parked in front of the main house, he ran to her side of the truck and led her out and up the stairs in record time. She sucked in deep breaths through her nose as she propped her hands on the nearest table.

"That was better than last time," she said.

"If you say so." He still felt like he could hurl at any moment.

She turned her head to the side, and her auburn hair fell down her neck like a waterfall. "Thank you."

Asher cleared his throat. "Don't thank me."

She straightened to her full height and moved closer to him, her green eyes locked on his. She seemed to move in slow motion, and by the time she'd taken two steps to close the distance between them, his heart was pounding like a war drum in his chest.

She was too close, and he was too tempted. All he wanted to do was wrap her in his arms and kiss her the way he had the first time he'd laid eyes on her. His chest rose and fell in steep waves as he remembered the way she'd crashed into him before sliding her soft lips over his.

He took a step back, and she stopped. Unfortunately, her intense gaze didn't release him.

"I do thank you. You taught me how to manage this crazy fear I've lived with for most of my life. I haven't conquered it or anything groundbreaking, but I'm getting better at facing my fear each time you lead me through the dark. Do you know what that means to me? The darkness has stolen so much from me." Her volume dipped to a whisper at the end.

He did, but would admitting it be the same as admitting his feelings for her? Every muscle in his body tensed.

Why couldn't she be just a friend? They shared so many interests. She loved music and art. She was funny and playful. She loved the Lord and the ranch.

Asher nodded and prayed she'd turn around and walk straight up the stairs to her room without looking back. He hoped she was stronger than him because he couldn't force his feet to move away from her if his life depended on it.

Haley did just what he'd hoped. She took a step back, and then another. "Good night. See you in the morning."

Asher tipped his invisible hat to her and waited until she was up the stairs and out of sight before crouching to the floor and hanging his head in his hands.

It wasn't supposed to be this difficult to avoid her. Having her here in the main house meant he would see her at least three times every day for meals.

Did Micah know how incredible Haley was? Did he even care? Asher hadn't heard from his brother since he left, but that wasn't unusual. Micah rarely spoke unless he was delegating ranch duties. He'd called their dad a few days ago to let him know it was taking longer than he'd expected to get the records for the herd, and he might be back by the end of the weekend.

Asher wanted to call his brother, but he also didn't. The thought of upsetting Micah after all he did to provide for the family made Asher's stomach twist into knots.

He stood, wrestling with his conscience. His cabin offered a night of taunting silence, but the least he could do was drive it out with a song. He had enough pent-up emotions to fill an album right now. Maybe he wouldn't feel so heavy if he bled them onto the page. His feelings for Haley stole his voice when she was around, but he could confess everything to the old walls of his cabin.

He didn't have a better idea, and morning came early when he had to wake up before the sun to check the herd.

Another day waited, offering more chances to see Haley and stoke the fire she'd kindled within him.

CHAPTER 19

HALEY

Haley shook hands with a white-haired woman with a wrinkled smile. "It's nice to meet you, Mrs. Simpson."

"You come back and see us," the woman demanded in the sweetest voice.

"I'll try. I've had a great time at the ranch."

Mrs. Simpson turned to Camille and wrapped her arms around her neck. Camille had to lean down to hug the woman's shoulders.

"You keep bringing those tourists to church, you hear?" Mrs. Simpson told Camille. "We have work to do for the Lord."

"Yes, ma'am." Camille brushed her dark hair behind her ear and adjusted her necklace. "It's always good to see you."

Camille had introduced Haley to a dozen church

members this evening. Haley was bursting with excitement to attend the Wednesday night service.

Haley, Camille, Maddie, and the Hardings lined up in two pews on the right side of the sanctuary and shifted left and right until everyone had enough room. Silas and Anita passed Levi back and forth through the first few worship hymns until he settled into Aaron's lap with a pencil and a bulletin. Asher sat next to Aaron, occasionally making a silly face at Levi. Haley sat at the end of the pew beside Camille and Noah.

Music was Haley's favorite way to praise the Lord. She prayed, she witnessed, and she confessed, but making a joyful noise filled her heart with the glory of the Holy Spirit. The entire congregation sang with all their might, and she felt surrounded by the love of Christ.

A few times, she tried to sneak a glance at Asher down the pew. He sang deep and loud, his voice full of conviction and truth.

Turning to face the altar again, she felt a slash of pain in her chest when she thought of Micah. He truly hadn't been the one for her, and the Lord had known that all along. Gabby was right. Haley had been chasing a ghost of love for years, but it was hard to force herself to step back from that instinct. The realization didn't make it any easier to temper her growing feelings for Asher.

Haley had been sure that Micah was interested

in her before she'd packed up and high-tailed it to Blackwater. She'd come here chasing love, but the Lord had closed that door for her. Now, she stood on the other side, waffling in her impatience as she waited for the Lord to open it back up again.

Micah hadn't given her a second thought, but Asher went out of his way to help her at every turn. His selfless acts tugged on her heartstrings daily, and all the signs seemed to point to Asher. After spending more time with him, he knew things about her that even her roommate didn't know.

More than that, looking at Asher felt like recognizing a reflection of herself. They shared so many beliefs and hobbies. He'd been helping her battle the toughest part of her life when he led her through the darkness and pointed her toward the light.

The Psalm.

Her brows drew together, and she stopped singing the hymn. It was a verse, but what if she *sang* it? She glanced at Asher down the pew, but he was focused on the words of the hymn in the book he held.

Haley knew in her heart that singing the verse would help her face her fear. She'd have to ask Asher if he'd be willing to help her try again. She wasn't ready to jump into the dark immediately because the thought of stepping outside at night still made her neck sweat.

After church, Asher waited with her until

everyone else had left before guiding her to his truck. When it came time to get out at the main house, she'd sung the Psalm a dozen times, and felt a fraction of the terror that usually gripped her bones in the darkness.

Once she was safely inside the house, Haley turned to Asher to whisper, "Thank you."

He nodded once as he hung his hat on the rack, but his eyes crinkled at the corners, conveying his pride with only a look.

Her chest filled with joy as she clomped through the meeting room in her heeled boots to catch up with Mama Harding. "Hey, can I help you with supper?"

"You're the guest," Mama Harding reminded her. "Just hang out, and I'll have it ready shortly."

"Will you please let me help?" Haley begged. "I want to learn your delicious ways."

Mama Harding opened the kitchen door and waved Haley in. "Oh, come on. It's just soup, but you can help me move the slow cookers to the serving table."

"Soup! Bless you. Does one of them happen to be the chili I loved?" Haley hadn't been discreet about her love of the white bean chicken chili.

"Your requests were noted. Can you stir them? I'll grab the crackers and cornbread."

She barely resisted tasting the soups as the smell

of spices filled her nose. "Will you please show me how to make these?"

Mama Harding lifted a nearby slow cooker and gestured for Haley to do the same. "We can actually start in the morning. I need to make some to freeze. Things have to keep running around here, even if I can't when I get sick, so I try to make it as easy on them as possible. None of them can spare a day, much less a whole week, cooking when there's other work to be done."

"That sounds great." Haley lifted a slow cooker filled with soup and followed Mama Harding out of the kitchen.

"We'll put them together in the morning after breakfast and set them out to cool just before supper. They should be cool enough to store in the freezer by bedtime." Mama Harding set the soup on the serving table and rested her hand on her hip. "Thank you for helping. You certainly don't have to. You're the guest."

Haley waved a hand and furrowed her brow. "Save the formalities. I'd rather be helpful than sit around twiddling my thumbs."

A few minutes later, everyone had steaming bowls of various soups, and Silas prayed the Lord would bless the food and the hands that prepared it. Levi kept everyone entertained during the meal. Gatherings with the Hardings felt like any given day in the

Meadows household, and Haley clung to the familiar camaraderie she'd experienced here. She would be sad to leave this place, and it was hard to believe she hadn't thought of her inevitable departure until now.

When everyone had finished eating and talking, Mama Harding stood and stacked Haley's empty bowl atop her own.

"I'll clean up," Asher said, standing to grab the nearby dishes.

Haley stood. "I need to get some work done tonight if I'm going to be in the kitchen with you all day tomorrow. I'll see you in the morning."

Everyone waved and said their good nights as Haley ascended the stairs to her room. She tinkered with the Blackwater Ranch website before diving into the most pressing job of the evening. She'd amassed quite a workload in the last few months, and she welcomed the distraction. She could easily get sucked into the ranching way of life here. The smell of the clean, morning air filled her with energy and excitement day after day.

After a long night of work and a few hours of deep sleep, Haley was ready to work. She skipped down to breakfast and greeted everyone with a peppy "Good morning."

As soon as talk of daily duties began, Mama Harding jerked her chin toward the kitchen, willing Haley to follow her.

"I'm coming." Haley stuffed her napkin onto the

empty dish and followed Mama Harding to the kitchen.

Asher wasn't far behind them with his arms loaded down with empty plates. "I'll clean up."

Mama Harding waved Haley over to a closed door in the side of the room. Haley looked back to see Asher picking up the first dish to wash before falling in line behind her teacher.

Inside, Mama Harding turned on the light to reveal floor-to-ceiling shelves stacked with canned goods, flour, corn meal, and any other food or ingredient imaginable.

The aroma of cooking spices filled the nook. "Wow. It smells amazing in here. If you can't find me later, I'm wallowing in the spicy goodness in the pantry."

Mama Harding chuckled. "Let's start with the taco soup. It's the easiest recipe in the book."

"Oh! Let me get my notebook. I want all the recipes."

"Go ahead," Mama Harding said. "I'll gather up the things we need."

"Be right back." Haley rushed up the stairs and grabbed a notebook she used to jot down song lyrics and poems along with her favorite pen. It was pale pink and had a fuzzy ball on the end that looked like the trufula trees in Dr. Seuss's *The Lorax*.

When Haley returned, Asher was drying his hands at the sink. His charming grin stopped her in her tracks and had her knees melting. He tossed the rag into a hamper and gave her a heart-stopping wink as he walked past her and out of the kitchen.

Stop gawking at him! You're such a dork.

Haley turned to lay her notebook on a nearby counter and came face-to-face with Mama Harding.

Haley gripped the sweater at her chest. "Anita, you scared me!"

Mama Harding's grin had *caught you* written all over it. "Mmhm. Sorry about that." She patted her hands on her apron. "Are you ready to start?"

Haley flipped through her notebook to a blank page. "Ready."

The next thirty minutes passed in a blur of ingredients, measurements, and temperatures. Haley's pen flew over the page as she noted everything Mama Harding said or did. Once the taco soup was mixed and cooking, Haley followed Mama Harding back to the pantry to document the things they would need for the white bean chicken chili.

They'd formed a system by the third round of soups, and they moved quickly through the prep. When the minestrone was heating in the slow cooker, Mama Harding leaned against the counter.

"I think we're about finished here."

Haley pointed to the skillets in the sink they'd used preparing the meats and vegetables for the soups. "I'll wash those."

Mama Harding picked up a drying rag and

joined Haley at the sink. "So, how's it going with my boy?"

Haley kept her gaze on the soapy pan and tried to hide her disappointment. "I'm not sure it's going at all. He hasn't messaged me on the Fated Mates site since he left." She focused on the dish as she decided to come clean. "And he kind of told me he wasn't interested in a relationship with me before he left." Haley shrugged. "I know he's busy, but I kind of came out here to get to know him better. He seemed like a stand-up guy, and I liked that about him."

"I knew Micah told you that before he left. I meant my other boy," Mama Harding said without looking up from her task.

Haley lowered the pan back into the soapy water. "What?" She wasn't sure which was more shocking, his mother's knowledge of Micah's dismissal before he left or the fact that she'd pegged Haley's growing feelings for Asher.

Mama Harding held out her hand for the next dish to dry. "I might have been born at night, but it wasn't last night. I see the way you two look at each other."

Haley handed over the soapy dish and Mama Harding rinsed it.

"You mean Asher?" Haley asked breathlessly.

"I love all of my sons, but they're all different. Micah thinks he needs a woman to run the ranch at his side, and he's searching high and low for a woman to spend his life with. He'll have to figure out that growing a relationship takes just as much time and effort as running this ranch." Mama Harding placed the last dish in the drying rack and leaned against the counter. "I also know that Asher is tearing himself up inside because no one has told him it's okay to care about you the way he does. I know when my boys are not themselves. He is good down to the bottom of his heart, and it's his way to put himself last."

Haley hung her head, unsure of what to say. "I was embarrassed to tell everyone that Micah wasn't interested in me, but I'm also scared of what could happen if I let myself fall for Asher. He's such a good guy, but my sister thinks I should wait before I jump into anything else. I agreed with her in the beginning, but now I'm not so sure."

Mama Harding put a hand over Haley's where it rested on the edge of the sink. "Asher's heart is full of love, but it's usually the friendly kind. Romantic love is something he doesn't understand yet, and I can see him struggling right now. His mission in life is to see everyone around him comfortable and happy, but this time, he thinks it comes at the cost of his own joy."

Haley whispered, "I'm sorry."

Mama Harding wrapped her arms around Haley's neck. "It's not your fault. It's a mother's job to help her kids learn to handle life's challenges, and I pray he'll understand when you're ready to tell him."

Haley huffed a sarcastic laugh. "Any idea when that should be? I came here chasing love, but now I'm hiding scared. I enjoy being with Asher. He's fun and kind, and he understands me better than almost anyone after only a short time. I promised myself I wouldn't rush into a relationship again, but that's exactly what I want to do with him. I just thought that if I didn't tell anyone about Micah breaking things off that I would have the space to take my time and find the man the Lord wants me to be with."

Mama Harding stepped back and grabbed a rag to wipe the counters. "I know you don't mean to hurt him, but I don't think any of us know the answer." She looked up and gave Haley a gentle smile. "I'll be praying, and we'll still love each other when it's all said and done."

Haley tucked her lips between her teeth to stop her chin from quivering. "I don't know what to do."

Mama Harding shook her head. "Don't say that. I believe you're doing the right thing by opening your heart to the Lord's will. Patience isn't a bad thing. It may be the best thing that has ever happened to you."

Haley wanted more than anything to believe the wise woman's words. She inhaled a deep breath and took her place beside Mama Harding cleaning up the kitchen. Haley had come here looking for love and a new beginning, and the more she knew the Hardings, the more she loved them.

She'd never been one to question herself, but she'd left Colorado searching for a future with Micah.

A week later, Asher was the only man she could see. He'd snuck into her heart, and she wanted him to stay there. Her sister had suggested she wait patiently, but what if she was meant to be with Asher? She desperately prayed it was the Lord's will, but how long would she have to wait to know for sure?

Haley had a lot to think about, and Mama Harding's words had only confused her even more.

CHAPTER 20

ASHER

Haley hadn't shown up to supper tonight, and Asher wasn't sure if his worry was valid. She could have decided to work or just been tired, but as he drove to his cabin, he had a sinking feeling that she needed someone to talk to.

He stepped into his cabin and started a fire in the fireplace. The temperatures were harsh tonight, and the heat needed to be circulating as soon as possible.

It was barely eight when he had settled in for the night, but a humming filled his bones and wouldn't let him relax. He wiped a hand over his face and scratched his jaw. He should just check on her already.

Grabbing his phone, he called Micah. Asher hadn't spoken to his brother since he left to get the bull, but his dad had given regular updates on the progress happening in Kansas City.

Micah answered with a direct, "Hello."

"Hey. Just checking in."

"Things are coming along, but nothing happens fast around here. The vet claims he forgot about our meeting, but I suspect it didn't get put on his schedule. He was out of town, and we had to wait for him to get back yesterday. He said he needed a day to get the paperwork together, and we have a meeting scheduled for tomorrow morning."

"That sounds promising. What about the rest of the herd?" Asher asked.

"No problems that I can discern. They run a pretty nice operation here."

"Good. Dad said you'll be home this weekend."

"Should be," Micah confirmed.

"I'm sure Haley will be ready to see you."

Micah paused. "What?"

"Come on. Please don't tell me you haven't talked to her since you've been gone." Truthfully, Micah wasn't the best at communication. He spoke up when something needed to be said, and he expected the same in return.

"Didn't she tell you? I had a little talk with her before I left, and I let her know she didn't need to wait around."

"What do you mean?" Asher asked.

"I only joined that dating site because I know

one day I'll be running the ranch. How am I supposed to meet someone, much less someone who would want to live on the ranch, if I hardly ever leave? She isn't just going to stroll in one day. Mom and Dad do such a great job of working together, and I think that's the best way to run a ranching business."

"Wait. Are you saying you want to get married so you'll have a business partner? That's the stupidest thing I've ever heard." Micah could be really dense sometimes.

"That's not exactly what I was saying, but I'm not getting any younger. Ranchers get tired and worn out long before they should. My good years might be behind me, and who is going to want an old, worn out cowboy?"

"Um, I don't think you're looking at this the right way."

Micah huffed. "I know. It makes sense in my head. I don't mean I just want a business partner. I mean I want someone to stand beside me through everything, like what Mom and Dad have."

"Okay, that makes a little more sense," Asher said.

"Are you saying Haley is still there?"

"Yeah. I thought she was waiting on you to get back." If she wasn't waiting on Micah, then what was she doing?

"Well, it doesn't have anything to do with me.

The dating site sounded like a good idea at the time, but I realized when she showed up that I may never have the time to get to know someone, much less marry them."

"Please act like you don't have five other ranch workers, a barn manager, a part-time ranch hand, and a full-time cooking staff to help you run this ranch."

"That's not what I'm saying. I just mean everything falls to me. The buck stops here."

"But you're still allowed to have a life outside of the ranch. I mean, Noah and Lucas do it just fine," Asher said.

"Yeah, and they also found women that happen to love living on a ranch. Trust me, women aren't lining up to be a rancher's wife."

Asher tapped his foot against the worn floor. "I'm sure there are some that would be okay with it."

"I hate to burst your bubble, but don't hold your breath for that one."

"Haley seems to like it here."

"Haley is... different. I could tell when I met her that we wouldn't work. She's way too smiley for me."

Asher couldn't agree with his brother's assessment more, but he also didn't like the way Micah always spoke as if the good things in life were out of his reach. "You could use a little sugar in your coffee. Don't sell yourself short."

"We aren't compatible. I could see it immediately. Anyone who would get in a car and drive to another state to meet a stranger on a whim, without even telling him, is not really my type. It made me realize that the dating site probably isn't going to cut it. We might work on paper, but real life is more than that."

Asher refused to get his hopes up that he might actually have a shot with Haley, but the possibility had his foot tapping faster and faster. "So, you're definitely *not* interested in Haley?"

"That's a definite no. She's nice, but her energy is exhausting. Just the little bit of time I spent with her that first night had me tired."

Asher wasn't sure what to say next, so he waited, hoping Micah would gift him some bit of information about the new bull he felt was particularly important.

"You like her?" Micah asked.

"What?"

"Haley," Micah said. "You like her." This time, it wasn't a question.

Asher cleared his throat. "I think she's great." That was safe. He also thought Camille and Maddie were great, but he didn't wake up in the mornings wondering when he'd get to hang out with them every day.

"I know you, brother. I can tell something is different in your voice when you say her name. I get it now. Why didn't you say something?"

Asher rubbed a hand over his hair and flopped back onto the couch. "We're just friends."

"If you just now found out that she and I aren't making a go of it, then I do believe she has only been your friend these last few weeks. But now that you know we're not together and nothing is ever going to happen between us, I bet that changes how you feel about her."

Asher swallowed hard. "I don't know."

"I know you wouldn't ever make a move on someone I was dating. I'm not mad. It really makes sense now. She's your type if you had one. It's not like I lost her. We weren't together to begin with."

"I have a type?" Asher asked. "And how do you know what she's like? You haven't even been here with her."

"Remember we've been chatting online for a month. We talked about a lot of stuff. Everything she mentioned that she loves is right up your alley. She's like you in a lot of ways. I can see how you would connect with her."

Asher paused. "You're really not mad?"

"I'm not. Relax."

"Okay, can I tell you that I kissed her when she first got here?"

The volume of Micah's voice rose considerably. "You what?"

"It was all an accident. She thought I was you, and I happened to be standing on the porch when she arrived. She came right up and laid one on me."

Micah laughed. Hard. Asher could count on two hands the number of times he'd heard his brother laugh, but it continued, and he hoped his brother hadn't lost his mind.

"That's the best thing I've heard all day. How did she think you were me?"

Asher began laughing too. "She had a picture of us, and she said you told her you were the one in the red shirt."

"I did."

"Dude. You are not the one wearing a red shirt in that picture."

Micah laughed again. "I remember sending that to her, and I really thought that one was red."

"That's what you get for thinking. She ran up to the porch and hit me with a big one."

"I have to tell Hunter. He'll get a kick out of this."

"Well, I sure did," Asher said.

"I bet you did. Was it any good?"

"Um, do you really want to know?" Asher taunted.

"Definitely not. Feel free to try that kiss again because I would bet you two are made for each other."

Asher tilted his head back and forth. "Probably."

"I have to go. Go get your girl, Casanova."

"You don't have to tell me twice. Drive safe."

Micah ended the call without a proper good-bye, but Asher didn't care. His mind was swirling with the new information.

Micah wasn't interested in Haley, and Haley wasn't interested in Micah.

Or was she? Was that why she hadn't told Asher? Had she told everyone except him? He flipped the phone over and over in his hands as his mind ran the gamut of possibilities.

Why hadn't she expressed any interest in him if she wasn't with Micah?

The last question hit him the hardest and had him questioning everything. Just because she wasn't interested in Micah didn't mean she would automatically be interested in Asher.

Maybe he needed to show her that he was interested first. He had his work cut out for him, and he was up for the challenge. He knew for certain that he wanted to be with Haley.

Tossing his phone onto the couch, he grabbed a clean pair of jeans and threw on a thermal undershirt and a flannel button-up. He needed to see Haley tonight.

CHAPTER 21
HALEY

When she finished packing the soup into freezer containers, Haley had thanked Mama Harding and asked to be excused from supper for the night. The emotionally jarring day had taken a toll on her, and she wanted to curl up in bed with a book.

After an hour, the silence grated against her skin, and she started calling her sisters. She spoke to Jess first, who seemed more certain of Owen's impending proposal. Then she called Beth.

"Hey. How's the ranch?"

"Just as beautiful as ever," Haley said.

"You sound glum."

"I'm fine. Just tired. I've been staying up late to work because there's so much to see around here. I just need a good night's sleep."

"Has Micah made it back yet?" Beth asked.

"No. He called his dad a few days ago and told him there were some tie-ups with the records. He might make it back this weekend."

"Are you excited to meet him?"

"I met him before he left. I just didn't get more than a couple of choppy conversations."

"Okay. Well, are you excited to get to know him?"

"I guess." Haley sighed. "Well, he actually told me before he left that he didn't think anything was going to happen between us. He didn't seem interested at all."

"What? Why didn't you tell me?"

"I don't know. I was hurt and upset. I just didn't want to call everyone in the family and relive it over and over."

"I'm sorry, Hales."

"It's okay. I'm not torn up about it anymore. I know he wasn't the man for me. I want to be with someone who is excited to spend time with me every day, you know? Someone who appreciates me and cares about me, and I want to feel that way about him too."

"You mean like Asher?" Beth asked.

"What? What made you think Asher?" Haley's heartbeat pounded in her ears.

"Because the two of you hit it off. You seemed really happy when he was around. You like the same things, you're both strong in your love for the

Lord, and I felt like you really cared about each other."

"We've only known each other for a few weeks."

"But you've spent every day together. You're both friendly and wear your heart on your sleeve. It could happen."

"I like Asher, but I'm not sure he feels the same about me." She probably liked Asher more than she should, but it was best to temper her drastic feelings.

"I think he does, but does he know about Micah?"

"No. Gabby told me I needed to take a break from trying to force relationships for a while."

"But have you forced anything with Asher?" Beth asked.

In truth, she felt comfortable with him in a way she hadn't with anyone she'd ever dated before. And maybe that was the difference. She wasn't dating him, and there wasn't any pressure to make sure he would like her. Right now, they were just enjoying each other's company, and it felt nice not to always be pushing for the next step and the next.

"No. I guess not. But he hasn't either, and I'm sure that's because he thinks I'm waiting on Micah to get back."

"I think you should tell him."

"Ugh. I think so too, but then it would be awkward. Oh hey, Asher, I came here to meet your brother, but he dropped me like a hot rock and I fell for you instead."

"Why not?"

"Because I should have said something before, and I didn't. If I say it now, it'll feel like I'm only saying it to bring my singleness to his attention."

"I think you're overthinking it," Beth said. "The next time someone brings up Micah, just say things didn't work out with him, but you've had a great time at the ranch anyway."

"I know. It's easy to assume it'll all work out perfectly when it's a conversation you're creating in your head. In real life, I'm going to flub it all up and make things weird."

"Probably," Beth conceded. "But you'll get it out in the open, and then you can see if Asher really wants to be your friend or if he feels the way you do"

A knock rapped on her door. "I've got to go. Someone is at the door."

"Talk soon. Love you."

"Love you too."

She disconnected the call and tossed her phone onto the bed as she went to check the door. Asher greeted her when she opened it. His lips barely tugged into a ghost of a grin.

"Hey. What are you up to?" she asked.

"Well, you didn't come down to supper, so I was just making sure you were okay."

She paused for a moment, caught off guard by his presence. "Thank you. I'm fine."

He jerked his head toward the stairs. "You hungry?"

She tilted her head back and forth, contemplating. "I could eat."

"Come on." He waited for her to take the first step before falling in line beside her.

"I'm in my PJs. You think anyone will care?" she asked.

"Nope. I'm the only one here, and I don't care."

"Your mom was very strict about meal times. I don't want to get on her bad side."

Asher cut a knowing glance at Haley. "Those rules don't apply to frozen pizzas."

"Yum! You brought pizza."

"Shh." Asher held his finger over his mouth. "We don't want to wake the neighbors."

"The closest neighbors are a dozen miles away," Haley pointed out.

Asher lifted his chin. "I said what I said."

She playfully shoved his shoulder as they walked down the stairs side by side. He lost his footing and grabbed onto the banister before he fell. They both burst into a fit of laughter and failed miserably at hiding the bubbly sounds.

"You're going to get me kicked out for keeping your parents up."

"If that was all it took to get kicked out, they'd have gotten rid of me a long time ago."

At the bottom of the stairs, he pointed to the table and disappeared into the kitchen. Haley sat at the table, and he came back minutes later balancing two pizzas in one hand and two bottles of water tucked under his arm.

He presented the meal with a flourish of his hand. "Dinner is served."

"It looks delicious. The presentation is top notch," she joked.

"Only the best for our one and only guest."

"I'm so honored to be doted on," she said.

The conversation halted as they scarfed down the pizzas. Haley hadn't realized how hungry she was until food was sitting in front of her. Her gaze locked with Asher's as they chewed, and his playful smile narrowed.

His voice was deep and smooth as he said, "It's okay to stare."

She swallowed the bite and almost choked on her laugh. "What?"

"It's the symmetry," he stated matter-of-factly.

"The what?" She'd given up trying to contain her laughter.

"I have good facial symmetry. It's visually appealing."

She tilted her head and gave him a once-over.

"Do you have to grease that head up to get it through the doorframe?"

Now it was Asher's turn to laugh. "I'm just saying, it's okay if you find me irresistible. It's common and perfectly natural. Nothing to be ashamed of."

"I'm not ashamed," she shouted in false outrage. His vanity was all in good fun.

He leaned over the table, and she felt her stomach drop when he whispered, "You're blushing."

"So, you think you're better than me because you're pretty?" She swatted his arm, but he caught her wrist. His grip wasn't tight, merely preventing her from the playful smack he deserved. When she looked up at him, the smile fell from his face.

"You're the most beautiful woman I've ever seen, and it has nothing to do with symmetry."

The room fell silent. She was frozen with his hand gently wrapped around her wrist. Her heart pounded inside her chest, racing, searching for the words to say.

He knew. He knew Micah wasn't interested in her. He had to. Was this a test? Was he trying to get her to tell him? Her brow furrowed as she warred with herself. This was her chance to tell him the truth, but the words were stuck in her throat.

Before she'd decided to tell him or leave it be, the tension left his body and he released her wrist. He brushed the pad of his thumb over the lines between her brows and let his fingertips drag down the side of her face and along her jawline.

She couldn't move. She couldn't breathe. No one had ever touched her so gently and with so much reverence. She'd barely felt the sweep of his skin across hers.

If it wasn't symmetry that drew her to him, it was chemistry. Exploding in a dangerous and violent eruption she couldn't control. Every cell in her body hummed at his proximity.

As quickly as he'd roped her in, he broke the connection and looked down to his pizza. "So, how are you holding up in this weather?"

She slowly inhaled a lungful, unsure of how to bring herself back to the reality of a conversation about the weather. Was he trying to put distance between them? Had they gone too far? The change of subject had her questioning everything. She tried to make her voice even. "It's okay. I'm used to the cold."

"Summer is nice. You'll get some good pictures then. And in the fall."

Her thoughts were still floating around his gentle touch, and she cleared her throat. "Yeah. I can't wait to see it when everything turns green."

Asher kept his attention on his food as he ate. "You'll love it."

She swallowed the truth like shards of glass. She

already loved it here. She loved the place and the work they did, and she wanted nothing more than to stay here with the happiness she'd found.

But she also loved the people here—Mama Harding, Camille, Lucas, Maddie, Levi...

And then there was Asher, who'd accepted her, quirky flaws and all. Looking at him felt like looking at a reflection of herself.

She would follow him into the dark, with the Lord at their side.

He'd seen her at her weakest, most vulnerable, and he'd lifted her up when she couldn't stand on her own.

The thought of leaving Blackwater Ranch twisted her stomach into a knot. But Asher made her wonder if a relationship could be this natural and uplifting.

Asher made the potential of a relationship look like spending forever with her best friend.

CHAPTER 22
ASHER

His adrenaline hadn't ceased its course through his body since he'd shown up at her door tonight. He hadn't planned to be so blunt with her, but he needed to know if she felt anything for him beyond friendship.

She'd been shocked by his confession, but she hadn't responded. Not that he expected her to, but he needed something to go on.

Friends or more? Friends or more?

They'd finally eased the conversation back to a safe topic, but he didn't want his time with her to end. Would he always crave more of her the moment she walked away? Would he always ache to kiss her every time he saw her?

Probably. And that would make it unbearable to watch her leave. He didn't have much time before Christmas, and nothing after that was certain. Well, today wasn't even promised, and the urgency of that realization spurred him into action.

"Do you want to go outside?"

Haley's eyes grew wide. "What? Why?"

He lifted a shoulder and let it fall casually. "I thought you'd like to see the stars. There aren't any clouds tonight."

She stared at him for a moment, waffling between her fear and her desire before whispering, "Yes."

He stood and offered her a hand. She studied it for a moment before she placed hers on top. Their hands fell into a comfortable hold, and he led her to the door where he held out his coat for her to slide her arms into. He didn't know if this was smart or foolish. The risk was high, but so was the reward.

He opened the door and then turned to her, grabbing her other hand in his. "I'll lead you. Close your eyes, and I'll tell you when to look."

She nodded and closed her eyes.

He took careful steps backward, tugging her hands toward the end of the porch. She followed him step by step into the dark. Was she repeating the verse? Did it help her like he'd hoped it would? Her hands weren't shaking, and he took that as a good sign.

He didn't rush her as he led her down the few steps off the porch. He stopped at a spot in the yard. The moon cast a silvery glow on her face, and he gently lifted her chin with his hand. With her eyes closed and a look of contentment on her face, she seemed at peace. The urge to seal his lips with hers grew with each passing second. His thumb traced the line of her jaw before he let it fall.

They were only friends, and they would only be friends until she said otherwise. He would respect her boundaries, but if he allowed himself to go anywhere with her, it would be too far.

He stood close enough to smell the scent of her shampoo, and he allowed his gaze to roam her face in the dim moonlight. Only a few inches separated their lips, and his breathing grew deep and ragged as he drank in every line of her face.

"Open your eyes."

Her lashes lifted, and her gaze settled on him. He hadn't been this close to her since the kiss they'd shared, and it would be so simple to repeat the motions their bodies already knew.

Everything inside him screamed to tell her. He wanted to be more than friends. He wanted to adore her and run headlong through life with her by his side.

He remembered their purpose and pushed his own desires back. "Look up."

Her gaze shifted up, and she gasped, bringing her hands to cover her mouth.

He rested his hand on her arm, letting her know he was right beside her. He would always be here.

When she lowered her chin, her eyes glistened with tears. "It's beautiful."

"You haven't seen it?" he asked.

"No," she whispered before looking up again to admire the heavens—God's far-reaching work of art. "Not in a long time."

He would be happy to stay right here, appreciating the beauty of the woman who had wrapped him up from the beginning. He didn't interrupt as she took her fill of the expansive night sky that she hadn't seen in years.

When she drew her attention back to him, he restrained every muscle in his body, willing them to let her lead him.

What do you want from me? Is it friends or the more we could be?

She slid one hand around his waist and then the other before erasing the space between them and resting her head on his chest. "Thank you."

Could she hear his heart beating violently in his chest? He wrapped his arms around her and hoped she could. If he couldn't admit the words out loud, he wanted her to listen to his heart and the beat that had her name written within it.

He tried to pinpoint the moment when she became his whole world, but he knew it had happened before tonight. His arms would always be open to her, waiting for her to find her comfort with him.

CHAPTER 23
HALEY

Haley stood in front of the small mirror in her room at the main house. How many days could she avoid Asher? With Mama Harding's help, she could continue to have her meals brought to her room.

She'd talked with Mama Harding the morning after Asher had shown her the stars, and his mother had understood Haley's need for space. She wanted to know her decision was the right one, and she'd spent the last few days praying and working.

She hadn't answered Gabby's calls since the night she'd had with Asher outside. He'd walked her inside, said good night, and walked away without chastising her for keeping a secret that wasn't a secret anymore. She hadn't admitted or confirmed anything, but he didn't need either of those things to know she was struggling with herself, and not because of any remaining attachment to Micah.

Her phone rang again, and she knew it was Gabby. She was pretty sure Beth had talked to her, or Gabby wouldn't be calling with such urgency.

Haley picked up the phone and fell back onto the soft bed. "Hey, sis."

"Haley, are you okay? Please answer my calls."

"I'm sorry. I'm okay, I just was avoiding you."

"I suspected as much, and I'm glad you're okay. Beth told me about Asher."

"Of course she did. Neither of you are helping at this point. I'm just as confused as ever."

"I know that now, but you left out a big piece of information when I suggested you take a step back from relationships."

Haley closed her eyes and let her sister get the lecture out of her system. "And what was that?"

"Asher. Why didn't you tell me about him? From what Beth told me, he sounds like he could be good for you."

"Or he could be the first man I ever truly love. The one who can break my heart."

Gabby huffed a long sigh. "*Or* he could be the one for you. Beth had only good things to say about him, and he sounds just like you—fun and quirky and loving."

Haley laid her arm over her eyes. "He's different, and I'm terrified."

Gabby said, "Different is good."

"In this case, different is amazing."

"Did you do what I said and pray about it?" Gabby asked.

"I did." Gabby didn't need to know that the prayers had been tearful and heartbreaking.

"And what do you know in your heart? What did the Lord tell you?"

"I feel like Asher could be the one, but I really don't want to mess this up."

"You can still take your time. Just let him know where you are. There's no harm in sharing your struggle. You've had enough rejection to last the rest of your life, and that was because those men weren't right for you. If Asher knows the real Haley Meadows and appreciates who you really are, that's something special."

"Once in a lifetime special," Haley echoed.

"Yes. I wish I could be there with you, but I think you need to do this on your own."

"I'll be fine. I promise." Haley wiped her eyes and sat up. "I'll talk to you soon."

"Love you."

"Love you too, Gab."

Haley took a deep breath and stood. She rummaged through her suitcase until she found a comfortable sweatshirt. She threw it over her T-shirt and adjusted the tie on her sweat pants before she walked out the door.

She turned on the hall light and tiptoed down the stairs. She left the upstairs hall light on and used what little light it gave her to make her way through the meeting room. It was plenty to discern the tables and chairs, and she made it to the door without issue.

With her hands flat against the door, she closed her eyes and prayed. *Lord, please walk with me. I need your strength to help me conquer this fear. In Jesus' name I pray, Amen.*

Haley unlocked the door and turned the knob. She could do this, but could she do it alone?

No, she wasn't alone. Her heavenly Father walked with her through the valley of the shadow of death and out into the cold Wyoming night.

When the door creaked on its hinges, she forced her eyes to remain open. Without Asher to lead her, she'd need to see what was ahead. Faint light shown through the windows of the meeting room out onto the porch revealing Asher sitting on the hard wood with a guitar in his lap. Did he know she'd be coming for him?

He looked up at her but didn't speak. She knew exactly what he was waiting for because she was waiting for her feet to move as well.

He kept his gaze locked on hers. "The dark can't hurt you."

She whispered, "I know."

With Asher and the Lord on her side, the darkness had lost its power over her. Asher had led her to an anchor who would never leave her.

Asher sat on the porch in front of her, as strong and mysterious as the darkness, but she knew he was the light. Just like her, he had the light of the Savior inside him, and she was drawn to him by the goodness of his bright heart.

The darkness couldn't steal the breath from her lungs or the blood from her heart anymore. Asher commanded her attention above all else in this moment, and she knew she would brave the choking night to hear him whisper a song in her ear.

She stepped over the threshold and forced air in and out of her lungs. She didn't have an excuse for this fear anymore, and she was willing to face it tonight.

Asher reached out his hand to her and she took it. His skin was ice cold, but she didn't let go.

He tugged gently on her hand, and she lowered to sit on the porch. She leaned her back against his and acclimated to her surroundings. There was enough light from the moon and the faint light through the windows to allow her to see shapes and shadows on the porch and across the yard.

After a moment, his fingers began to move over the strings of the guitar, and she closed her eyes to listen. She'd always loved the beautiful sound of music, but tonight, she wanted to feel it.

A few heartbeats later, Asher began to sing, and

she felt the vibrations of his voice on her back, seeping into her heart. The song stilled her, begging her to listen intently. It was an original, she could tell, and it felt like a gift. A song for her ears alone. It was a reminder of the joy they'd found, the possibility of more, and a realization of all the things that could slip through their fingers if they lost this.

She wrote the words on her heart, committing each one to memory.

> You might be putting on a show,
> But I can't seem to let you go.

H e loved her. She could feel it. The way he felt about her was equal to the love she felt for him.

She'd thrown her heart into the world, begging someone to catch it and give it a home. Now, she held it close, protected until she could give it to him.

> I just never thought it would be you.

Wasn't that the truth. When she'd packed up for Wyoming, she'd expected to fall in love with a man she hadn't met yet. But this... It was as unexpected as she always hoped love would be.

A single tear slipped down her cheek. What a pair they made, connected by their reaching hearts.

When the song was over, she whispered, "Asher."

"Hm."

How did she tell him she loved him when they weren't even a couple? This was what her sister meant when she said it was okay to slow down.

"That song was beautiful."

She wiped the cold tear from her cheek and stood to her feet. "Good night."

"Good night, Haley."

She stepped inside and leaned against the door, willing her racing heart to steady. Was it fair to tell him now? Christmas was only a few days away, and she needed to leave the day after tomorrow to make it home for Christmas Eve with her family.

He may have feelings for her, but were they enough to last through a long-distance relationship?

Her heart felt heavy as she made her way up the stairs.

CHAPTER 24
HALEY

Haley didn't necessarily avoid Asher over the next few days since they saw each other at mealtimes, but she hadn't had much time to spare. With Christmas only a few days away, any website glitches her clients experienced needed immediate attention, and many of them requested expedited updates or changes.

She welcomed the business, and it kept her mind off Asher. If she thought about him for too long, she would be confessing her undying love in an instant. But Gabby's wisdom still rang true. Haley *did* need to be patient and sure before rushing headlong into a new relationship, especially one that had the potential for a future.

After supper, Asher cut his eyes toward the door, but she shook her head. His eyes narrowed in concern, so she gave him a reassuring smile.

"Hey, Camille. Can I ride with you tonight?" Haley asked loud enough that Asher could hear. She knew Noah was working at the fire station tonight.

"Sure." Camille stood and grabbed her empty plate along with Haley's. "We can leave in just a few."

Everyone else took their empty plates to the kitchen, and Haley snuck over to Asher's side.

"I thought I might try doing this on my own." She cut her glance to the floor. There was a possibility she could end up panicking in front of Camille, but her friend would understand.

Asher's gaze locked with hers when she looked up. He was studying her, making sure she was okay and also silently offering her his help if she ever needed it.

Haley whispered, "I can do it."

Asher nodded. "I know. It's just that you're leaving soon, and I was hoping I'd get to spend some more time with you."

She was leaving tomorrow. Christmas was only a few days away, and she had to make the long drive back to Colorado. Her throat constricted every time she thought about leaving. "I'll see you tonight."

Asher's mouth quirked up on one side in a heart-stopping grin. "Save me a dance?"

Oh, if he only knew. If she had her way, he could have every dance. "Of course."

With that, Asher turned and walked out the

door. He'd need time to set up if he intended to play tonight, and she wished she was going with him.

Camille showed up a minute later, and they grabbed their coats and scarves before heading out the door. Camille stepped out first, and Haley rushed to prepare for the coming darkness. Thankfully, Asher had turned on the porch light when he left, and it lit up the porch and the area just beyond. She still prayed and sang the Psalm in her head as she stepped through the thin layer of snow to the car.

Once in the vehicle, Haley knew she'd have to explain a few things if she was going to make it through this ride. "Do you mind if we leave the cab light on?"

Camille turned to look over her shoulder as she backed out. "Not at all."

"I'm sort of afraid of the dark." It was a gross understatement. "It's more of a crippling phobia than just scared of the dark."

"Really? Why didn't you say so?" Camille asked as she turned to start down the straight path out of the ranch.

"Well, it's kind of embarrassing." Haley tried to focus on the conversation, but she was having trouble controlling her breathing.

Camille laughed. "Everyone is afraid of something. Asher is terrified of spiders."

Haley nervously chuckled. "He told me. Is it

really that bad?"

"Oh, yes. At least he can laugh about it. I get the feeling that isn't the case here."

"Not at all. It's debilitating." Haley picked at her fingernails in her lap. "Asher has been helping me."

Camille sighed. "That sounds just like him. He's a helper. He can't stand to see someone uncomfortable or in need."

"I know," Haley whispered.

A silent moment filled the car before Camille confessed, "Mama told me about Micah."

Unsure of what to say, Haley didn't speak.

"I'm sorry that it didn't work out with him, but I'm also not sorry because I think Asher is perfect for you," Camille said.

Haley kept her gaze down as she whispered, "Me too."

W hen they arrived at Barn Sour, Camille met Haley at the front of the car and wrapped an arm around her shoulder as they walked in together. She only felt a faint remnant of the crippling fear that she'd known only a few weeks ago.

They fell into the comfort of the local scene as Camille spoke with a few people she knew and introduced Haley. The people of Blackwater seemed to know and love each other as they offered helping hands and promised prayers. She loved the familiarity here, and knew she'd be planning a trip back to Blackwater as soon as she could.

Each time her gaze found Asher in the crowd, he was looking at her. Heat crept up her spine as his brown eyes called to her.

She'd been talking with Camille and Maddie in a booth for fifteen minutes before something caught Camille's eye in the crowd.

"Micah is here."

Haley jerked around in her seat to see, and she spotted him immediately. A few men gathered around him to talk. He looked the same as she remembered, but she also had the certain feeling that he was a stranger. Funny that she had come here thinking she already knew him. Her whole intention for coming here sounded crazy and impulsive. She raised the back of her hand to her face, covering her giggle.

Asher's booming voice rose over the chatter of the crowd. "Good evening, ladies and gentlemen."

Haley drew her attention to the stage. Asher sat on a barstool with a guitar resting in his lap. His easy smile had her blood pumping wildly through her veins, and she rested a hand on her heart, willing it to settle.

"I have a few songs for you tonight, and I'll be taking requests later." His fingers strummed against the strings, and a few screams and whistles filled the small space.

Camille stood and tugged on Haley's arm. "Come on. Let's dance."

She led Haley to the dance floor. The beat of the song vibrated in her bones, coaxing movement from her muscles.

The women danced through each upbeat song and took a break for water during the slower ones.

When Asher began the slow tune of "I Cross my Heart" by George Strait, Haley returned to the booth where Micah stood talking to Maddie.

Haley stepped up next to him and decided to rip the bandage off. "Hey."

"Hey. It's good to see you again."

"You too. Did you have a good trip?"

Micah leaned against the side of the booth and scratched his head. "Got the bull. I guess that's a job well done."

Haley grinned. His response fit the mold of what she now knew about him from his family. "Good. Glad you're back."

A few minutes later, Asher set down the guitar and joined them at the booth. He greeted his brother with a knowing look and a nod. Haley's gaze drifted back and forth between the two men, and she knew Micah had been the one to tell Asher that he'd let her down gently before leaving. She wondered if Asher had come clean about the kiss too. Oh, to be a fly on the wall during that conversation.

Haley spotted Donna wiping the bar and excused herself to speak to the owner.

"Donna."

"Hey! I'm so glad you're back." Donna wrapped Haley in a brief, intense hug.

"I'm glad to be back. Would you mind if I played a song? Just one."

Donna's eyes grew wide. "Not. At. All." She emphasized each word with a pause between. "Let me introduce you." Donna threw the rag behind the bar and grabbed Haley's hand, leading her to the stage.

"Hey, everyone. This is Haley Meadows, and she has a special treat for us tonight. Let's give her a warm welcome."

Everyone in the building hooted and clapped as she gave a small wave and stepped up to the mic.

"Hey. I'm Haley, and I want to thank Donna for letting me sing you this one song." She picked up Asher's guitar and settled herself on the stool. She propped the guitar on her legs as she adjusted the mic. "I've been staying at Blackwater Ranch, and I've had the best time here. I wanted to share the latest song I wrote with you to say a huge thanks for being so welcoming."

She touched a few strings on the guitar to make sure she was ready. She'd practiced a few nights this week, and she felt confident.

"This song is really for someone special. I met a

lot of wonderful people here, but one of them really changed my life." She cut a glance to Asher standing propped against a nearby table with his arms crossed over his chest. She forced herself to look away from him. If she thought about it too much, she would second guess everything, and she was committed now.

Her fingers found the strings she needed, and she began to play the slow tune of her newest song. She closed her eyes, and the strum of the guitar vibrated in her chest. Her racing heart had settled into the comfort of the song by the chorus.

> I never thought we'd go this far,
> But you showed me the stars.
> In a world of black on white,
> You lead me into the light.
> You're the only one who knows,
> I'm a heart without a home.
> A heart without a home.

She played and sang the rest of the song, putting her all into the words she desperately needed to confess. She'd prayed over these words and toyed with them for days, and she felt called to sing them —for Asher and everyone else who would listen.

After she played the last chord, the quiet restaurant exploded into applause. She rested the guitar in the stand and made her way off the stage. A few people stopped her to tell her how much they loved the song, and she smiled and thanked each of them.

When she stopped at Asher's side, the intensity of his expression stole her breath. The muscles in his jaw twitched, and his gaze dropped to her mouth.

"Haley! That was amazing." Donna grabbed Haley's arm and bounced with excitement. "You have to play more."

Haley tried to focus on the kind owner who had allowed her to sing the song God had put on her heart for Asher. "Thank you so much, but I'm leaving in the morning."

"No! You can't. Are you coming back?"

Haley shrugged one shoulder. "I hope so."

"You know where to find me." Donna wrapped her in a hug and rocked her from side to side.

"Thanks. I'll miss you."

Haley said her good-byes to Donna and turned back to the table where her friends waited anxiously.

"Haley." Camille drew out her name to emphasize her sincerity. "That song was amazing. Did you really write that?"

Haley nodded.

Maddie cupped her cheeks. "It was so pretty."

Haley took a deep breath and turned to face

Asher, but he wasn't standing beside her anymore. "Where did Asher go?"

Micah pointed toward the door. "He left while you were talking to Donna."

"He left?" Haley felt her heart tumble. Had she made a mistake?

Camille pointed toward the stage. "He couldn't have gone far. His guitar is still here."

Haley eyed the door leading to the dark parking lot. "I'll be right back."

Her prayer was quick and pleading this time. *Lord, please guide my words. Please help me to face Asher and the darkness. I feel like you led me here to him, but I don't know what to do.*

She grabbed the door handle and pulled before she could change her mind. A dim light on each side of the exit lit the small entryway, but the parking lot beyond faded into darkness.

Looking both ways, she didn't see Asher. With a deep breath that froze inside her lungs, she stepped around the right side of the building searching for his truck.

A dark figure leaned against the wall on the side of the restaurant, and she knew it was Asher by his stance. His head was lowered, and his arms were crossed over his chest.

"Hey." The word was quiet as she forced it through her constricting throat.

Asher looked up. When he saw her, he walked to

her and placed a hand on her back, leading her toward the entrance. He didn't guide her around the corner, but at least they were in the circle of the entrance light.

"What are you doing out here?" he asked. Panic laced his words.

"You left." She begged her words not to quiver, but she was holding back the tears that desperately wanted to escape.

Asher rubbed a hand over the top of his head. "I wasn't leaving. I was just getting some air."

"Freezing air?" As she said the words, a breath cloud formed between them.

Asher nodded. "Your song—"

"I'm sorry I didn't tell you about Micah. I was embarrassed that I'd come all the way out here to meet a man that wasn't interested in me at all."

Silence filled the air between them until he asked, "And?"

"And I wanted to stay. I wanted to get to know everyone and see the ranch and just have some time for me without the pressure and pitiful looks from everyone." Haley twisted her finger to pick at the nail. "And then I didn't want to leave."

She wanted nothing more than to know this moment—this bond she'd found with Asher—would stay forever. She looked up at him, and the tears refused to be stopped. "I don't want to leave." Her voice broke, and she leaned into him.

He wrapped her in his arms, and she let the tears fall. The ache in her chest grew, slid up her throat, burned her eyes, and fell down her face. He held her until the tears slowed, and then he began to slowly rock, shifting his weight from one side to the other.

"I said I'd save you a dance," Haley whispered against the corduroy of his thick coat.

"Is this my dance?" he asked.

"Do you want it to be?"

She felt the scruff of his cheek brush against her hair as he nodded.

"Yeah. I do."

She lifted her head from his chest to face him. She studied his face in the dim light. His dark eyes were beautiful and bold, and she wanted to remember everything about this moment.

His thumb slowly brushed over the line of her jaw, down her neck, and back up to cup her cheek and thread into her hair.

He rested his forehead against hers and whispered, "If you're afraid of this, you're not the only one."

Her heart reached for him, and she wanted to hold onto him—this moment—for the rest of her life.

But she was leaving in the morning, and they hadn't had enough time. She'd spent her time here wallowing in indecision, and now it seemed too late. If they laid everything out in the open now, they'd be beginning a relationship four hundred miles apart. The soonest she could be back in Blackwater was the beginning of January.

His dark gaze fell to her lips. "I shouldn't kiss you. I shouldn't even want to kiss you." He swallowed. "But I do. I want to so bad."

He was so torturously close that she could feel the heat of his breath on her face.

Her words were so quiet, she wondered if she'd said them at all. "I'll come back."

His head slowly moved up and down, and his gaze was intent on her. "I want you to come back."

"This isn't the last dance. We can have more." She could hear the panic rising in her voice. Would he be willing to wait?

She would wait. She could wait for Asher Harding for a thousand lifetimes.

She wanted to kiss him. She wanted him to kiss her first, but she also knew it wasn't fair to either of them. She'd be leaving in the morning, and one kiss would be followed by days of loneliness. One kiss would only make things harder when it came time to leave in the morning.

She didn't want kisses. She wanted Asher—his love, his generosity, and his faithfulness.

Maybe she could have all of those things, but not tonight.

"Asher."

They both turned to see Camille standing beneath the light at the entrance.

Camille pointed into the bustling building. "I hate to interrupt, but it's time for your next set."

Asher let his arms fall from around her and rested his hand at the small of her back to lead her inside.

Haley didn't move. "I'll be in soon. I just need a minute."

Asher's gaze was scared and unsure. "Are you sure?" He was reluctant to leave her in the dark alone.

"I'm sure."

He stepped away from her but turned to keep her in his sight until he disappeared into the building.

When the doors closed behind him, she lowered her head and said the words that begged to be released.

"I love you."

She covered her mouth and let the tears fall. She'd been chasing love her whole adult life, but she had no idea it would be so painful.

The chord of Asher's first song reached beyond the walls and into the parking lot where she cried.

CHAPTER 25

ASHER

Asher stood outside Haley's door before the sun came up. He studied the paper in his hands as he turned it over, unsure if he was making the right decision.

The quiet of the hallway seeped into his skin and left him itching for sound of any kind. He couldn't think when there was so much silence. He scratched the back of his neck and made a quick decision before he chickened out. He wanted to give her the note, but he also hoped he wasn't breaking his own heart in doing it.

He slid the paper under the door of her guest room and walked back down the stairs empty handed. There was no going back now. She was leaving in a few hours, and Christmas was two days away. She deserved more than the simple gift he'd given her, but if anyone could appreciate the present, it was Haley.

His mother waited at the bottom of the stairs. Her hip rested against the serving counter, and Asher tried to recall the last time he'd seen his mother so still. Other than church, she hadn't stopped to rest in years.

"Hey. Everything okay?" he asked.

"I don't know. Is it?"

Asher shrugged.

"Is she leaving?" his mother asked.

Asher shrugged again. He wasn't sure he could use his words right now. His throat felt white hot and dry.

His mother tilted her head, and her expression was soft. "Did you ask her to stay?"

"Not in so many words, but yes." The note was more of a confession, but he wasn't sure he could verbalize it.

His mother wrapped her thin arms around his shoulders. "I love you, son. I hope she stays."

"Was it wrong to ask her to?" he whispered.

"I don't think so. Haley knows what's at stake. I believe she'll understand. I've been praying for the two of you, and I think you would be good for each other."

Asher released her from the hug. "Thanks, Mom."

"You heading out?"

"Yeah. I'll try to make it back before breakfast. I have a few things to do so I can see her before she leaves."

"If she leaves."

"Mom, you know she has to go home for Christmas at least. I don't want her to miss that time with her family, no matter how much I want her to stay here."

"I know."

He kissed his mother's cheek and headed out into the freezing December morning. The uncertainty of the day had his adrenaline pumping. He wanted more time with Haley, but she had a life in Fort Collins. They could do the long-distance thing, but he would miss her. It was selfish of him to want more of her, and he would choose to love her four hundred miles away over nothing at all.

What if she didn't want him at all? He thought she did after hearing her song, but maybe she thought they were better off as friends. He wasn't sure if he could handle that rejection, but he might not get a choice. There were so many things he wanted to share with Haley, his life included, and the thought of missing out on a lifetime of laughter with her had his jaw clenching in fear.

Micah's truck was parked in front of the north hay barn when Asher arrived. At least he wouldn't have to talk about it. Micah had the emotional depth of a teaspoon, and he was the last one to hash out mushy feelings.

Inside the barn, Micah was changing the attachment on the skid steer. Asher set his eyes on the tractor just past the large opening on the other side of the barn. If they teamed up to do the feeding this morning, he could get back before breakfast to see Haley.

Micah stood and propped on the machine. "Hey, you okay?"

Asher stopped. "Yeah. Why?"

"I don't know. You usually hum or whistle or something." Micah narrowed his eyes. "Is it because Haley is leaving?"

Asher thought he'd be spared the feelings talk, but it seemed he needed to drive the stake into the ground. "She's leaving after breakfast. I just want to get back in time to see her before she goes."

"Did the two of you talk things out? Or is she just going to leave?" Micah asked.

Asher propped against the other side of the skid steer. "I don't know. I spent so much time thinking she was off-limits, and now it feels like we don't have enough time to even start something before she leaves. I just wish I had more time."

"Why don't you take some time off and go see her after the new year?" Micah suggested.

Asher rubbed his chin. "I could do that. I'll ask her about it at breakfast."

"You think she's interested?" Micah asked as he locked the attachment in place on the machine.

"I think so. I almost kissed her last night, but I wasn't sure if that's what she wanted. I mean, she's leaving today. Everything gets harder when we're that far apart."

"Almost only counts in horseshoes and hand grenades. Her song last night made it pretty clear that she has feelings for you, and the two of you could make it work long distance until things get more serious. Then you worry about the distance and the future."

Asher checked the lock on his side of the attachment. "I know. That's what I'm hoping she'll say. I left her a note this morning telling her everything. It'll all be out in the open when she wakes up."

Micah climbed into the machine and secured the safety belt and bar. "That's all you can do." He reached above his head to start the engine, and the rumble filled the huge barn.

Asher headed to his own machine and climbed on. He was nervous and anxious to get back to the main house, and within minutes he had the large round bail skewered on the hay spear. It wasn't a far ride on the tractor to the nearest feeder, and Dixie ran along beside him in the snow as the sun broke over the horizon. He usually sang while running the tractor, but his thoughts were louder than the engine this morning.

He dropped the bale into the cage and climbed out of the tractor cab. The winter wind burned his eyes, and he pulled his neck gaiter over his mouth and nose while he cut the twine around the bale. With the twine wrapped around his hand, he stepped back onto the tractor.

He reached into the cab to pull himself up, but the hand wrapped in twine slipped off the bar he'd grabbed. He extended his other hand, grabbing for anything he could for balance, but he was falling back and his gloved hand barely touched the handle on the door before it slipped off. He fell to the ground hard and fast, landing with a jarring thud on his back. His lungs were screaming as he tried to gasp for air, but nothing happened. Panic gripped him as he realized he couldn't breathe—in or out.

Looking up at the baby-blue sky, he willed his heart to calm and kept trying to push air out or suck it in. If he couldn't make it happen soon, he'd die in this field alone and wishing he'd had more time.

He closed his eyes and silently prayed. Every word was urgent and begging.

When he'd repeated the same prayer for deliverance half a dozen times, his chest began to rise and fall in shallow measures. One by one, his breaths lengthened, drawing in the freezing air before pushing it out to grab for more. But with the air came the pain, and he squeezed his eyes closed against the onslaught.

This time, he began a new prayer. He could handle broken ribs, but a broken spine would change his life forever. The ranch couldn't afford to lose him. His family needed him, and he needed more time to grow old. He desperately wanted more time before the Lord called him home.

He wanted Haley. Today and every other day, and he wanted to be around long enough to love her.

With the deepest breath he could manage, he slowly moved one arm and felt around for the pocket of his coat. He focused on the air filling his lungs and pushing back out as he gently pulled his phone from the pocket.

The sun cast bright beams of orange across the clear sky as he lifted the phone. Without moving his neck, he cut his eyes as far down as he could and found the buttons to call Haley.

She answered on the second ring. "Hello."

"The north pasture." It took every ounce of strength he had to utter the words, and he hoped it would be enough. The tractor was still running, drowning out every other sound in the area.

"Aaron is right here. What's wrong? Do you need an ambulance?" she asked.

"Yes." Asher wasn't sure how extensive the injuries were, but if there was any internal bleeding or a spinal fracture, he'd need professional help.

"I'm coming."

Haley disconnected the call, and Asher let his arm fall too quickly, sending a stabbing pain up his arm and down his back.

Noah and Lucas were on duty at the fire station today, and he trusted his brothers with his life. A life he desperately wanted to be able to spend with Haley by his side.

The cold snow at his back was seeping through his coat, and he let the numbness fill his bones while he prayed. He needed to see Haley again. He needed to hear her voice again. He closed his eyes and allowed a vision of her auburn hair and green eyes to drive out the pain.

CHAPTER 26

HALEY

Haley rolled over in bed before sunrise and pulled the blanket over her face. She'd endured a night of fitful dreams filled with running and darkness, and she wasn't ready to get up.

In fact, she didn't want to face the day at all. She wanted to see her family for Christmas, but she also wanted to spend the holiday with the Hardings. They'd been so good to her, and she'd grown to love them in the last few weeks.

Love. Wasn't that the real reason she didn't want to leave? Asher had stormed into her life and changed everything.

She'd come here chasing love, and she'd found it —with Asher, his family, and the ranch. Was it selfish of her to have a wonderful family who loved her and still wish to be a part of what the Hardings had?

Christmas was in two days. The Meadows family had scattered a little over the years, but they always made it back to Mom and Dad's for Christmas.

Haley buried her face in the flannel sheet and huffed a warm breath. "Dear Lord, please guide my heart. I feel drawn to Asher and this place, but I want to follow Your path for me. Is this it? Is this my future?" She pulled the covers down and saw the first sign of the sun creeping through the window before closing her eyes again. "Thank You for letting me spend this time here. I think it was good for me. I needed these people. And please help me to be patient. In Jesus' name I pray. Amen."

She threw off the covers and rolled out of bed. The day was going to happen whether she liked it or not, and she'd rather face it with pants on.

First order of business was to pack. She still hadn't mastered sleeping in complete darkness, so the first thing she grabbed was her night-light. When she reached to unplug it from the outlet, a strip of white on the floor caught her eye.

She picked up the paper and studied it. Her name was written in capital letters on the folded paper. The bold handwriting made her smile. She hadn't seen anything Asher had written before, but she smiled at the pen strokes. She'd guess the dark lines were Asher's any day.

When she opened it, there were two pages folded together.

. . .

Haley,

I'll be back before you leave today, but I wanted to leave you a note because I'm not brave enough to say these things to you in person yet. I can't let you leave without telling you how much you mean to me.

Micah told me that the two of you aren't talking anymore. Actually, he said the two of you haven't been talking since he left. When I found out, I can't tell you how relieved I was. Since the moment you kissed me, I've had feelings for you that I definitely shouldn't have for my brother's girlfriend, and I've been torturing myself over it.

So when he told me to go for it and tell you how I feel, I felt like I could finally be honest with you—and myself. I loved you when you needed help in the dark, that night under the stars, and when I heard the song you wrote. I knew there was so much more between us that we were afraid to admit.

But I was also worried because you hadn't said anything. I wondered if that meant you weren't interested in anything more than a friendship between us.

Now, it's time for you to go, and I haven't told you how much I love you. I've wanted to say it so many times, but I was afraid it would change us. I've never felt this way about anyone, and I know it's because you're special. I'm pretty sure God sent you to me. I've been praying for someone to spend my life with, and then you showed up. I think I always knew it was you.

I know you want to spend Christmas with your family, but I'm going to miss you. I hope you'll come back to me soon because I'm going to need two lifetimes to show you how much I love you.

Love,

Asher

P.S. Pretend I didn't tell you I loved you for the first time in a note. I want to say it in person.
P.P.S. I wrote you this song.

Haley read the letter again, hanging on every word that told the story of his love.

He loved her.

When she reached the end of the letter the second time, she hurriedly flipped to the second page. The structured verses of a song filled the white space, and she wanted to devour the song and savor it at the same time. She brushed the pad of her thumb over the title.

I Always Knew it was You.

She wiped the silent tears from her cheeks as she read every word. A shaky laugh escaped from her chest and past her smile. It was Asher. He was the one she'd been waiting for her whole life.

She laid the papers on the bed and rushed to throw on pants and a few layers. If Asher was out on the ranch, she wasn't going to wait around for him this morning. Patience still wasn't her strong suit, and she'd held back for too long.

Slipping on her boots, she tightened the laces and tied them in a speedy bow before grabbing the papers on her way out the door.

Several family members had already arrived for breakfast, and she searched the room for Asher. She still hadn't spotted him when she reached the bottom of the stairs. Her phone was ringing, and she pulled it from the back pocket of her jeans.

She continued scanning the room and answered the call without looking at the screen.

"Hello."

"The north pasture."

Cold fear shot down her spine at Asher's forced words. Something was wrong. She could hear the pain, and it sliced through her heart.

She looked for the closest Harding and moved to stand by Aaron. "Aaron is right here. What's wrong? Do you need an ambulance?"

Aaron stopped what he was doing and gave her his full attention, awaiting instruction.

"Yes."

The word was little more than a breath, but it spurred her into action. "I'm coming."

She hung up and said to Aaron, "He's in the north pasture. He needs an ambulance."

Aaron moved quickly, and Haley slapped the papers onto the table before following him. Fear rose in her chest as she sprinted to the door.

She stopped on the porch where Aaron was shoving his boots onto his feet.

Aaron stepped off the porch and pointed to his truck. "Get in."

When they were both settled into the cab, Aaron called for an ambulance. Haley listened as Aaron answered their questions, but they both knew so little about what had happened to Asher or his condition.

Aaron stayed on the phone with dispatch as they bounced over the uneven terrain to a part of the ranch she hadn't seen since she arrived weeks ago. Asher had brought her here. She'd taken photographs of the beautiful scenery and wrestled with herself and her feelings for the man she'd just met.

Aaron kept his eyes on the path ahead and pulled the phone from his face. "I don't know how bad off he is, but Noah, Lucas, and Jameson will be here soon. They'll know what to do."

Haley kept quiet. There wasn't anything she could do right now, and she felt a pang of solidarity with Mama Harding. Sending the people you love out into the world every day was wonderful and heartbreaking at the same time.

Aaron spotted the tractor at the top of a slight rise and pushed on the accelerator. Haley scooted to the edge of her seat and scanned the area, but she couldn't see him.

Her gaze followed Aaron's finger as he pointed to the tractor. "He's on the ground, but the tractor is idling, so that's good news."

She needed good news right now. She needed

good news and Asher in her arms. Closing her eyes, she prayed for the Lord to walk with them, to put His healing hand on Asher, and to give her the strength to endure this worry for the safety of the man she loved.

Haley opened the truck door before Aaron had shifted into park. She jumped out and ran for Asher and the life she wanted. She ran toward her heart.

Aaron yelled behind her, "Don't move him!"

Haley slid to a stop in the slushy snow beside Asher. He lay flat on his back and only his eyes moved to look at her as she leaned over him, scanning for blood.

"I'm here. I'm here. What happened?" she asked quickly.

Asher reached for her hand with a wince, and she took it, wrapping his gloved hand in hers. She'd run out of the house so fast, she'd forgotten her jacket and gloves.

His voice was low and deep as he said, "I fell. I think it's just ribs, but it hurts to move on my own, and I don't want to chance it."

"No, don't move. They're on their way. Just try to relax. I'm here."

Aaron ran up and threw a thick blanket over Asher's body. "How long have you been here?"

Asher closed his eyes. "Not long, but too long." He was shaking with cold or shock.

Haley leaned over him and brushed her hair out of her face. "I love you, Asher. I love you. I want to stay. Please..." She let the sentence hang in the air around them as she ran a hand over his face. "I love you." The words fell in a whisper between them, and she bit her lips between her teeth as a tear dropped onto his coat.

Asher squeezed her hand and winced. "I love you too. I'm alive, and that's what matters. When my brothers get here, they'll know what to do."

She shook her head as fresh tears slid from her eyes and fell like tiny diamonds in the freezing air. While her eyes were closed, she prayed. One hand held Asher's and the other rested on his chest, celebrating each steady rise and fall. The snow beneath her melted, soaking the bottom half of her pants and reminding her that this was real, not a dream.

Aaron killed the engine on the tractor, and they heard the faint siren of the approaching ambulance. He moved to signal their location as help arrived.

Noah and Jameson jumped out of the ambulance as Lucas's truck parked nearby. Mama Harding rushed to where Haley crouched beside Asher, and they both moved back to allow the paramedics to assess him.

Noah, Lucas, and Jameson were dressed the same in the fire department uniform, and they worked like a well-oiled machine as they checked

Asher's condition and carefully moved him to the backboard.

Haley held tight to Mama Harding's hand, drawing strength from the matriarch as two of her sons worked to save another.

"Haley." Asher's voice was strained, and a wince followed his shout.

She left his mother's side and moved to stand beside the gurney. "I'm here." She wrapped his hand in both of hers, thankful for the anchor when fear filled her thoughts.

"Don't worry. I'm going to be okay," he assured her.

Mama Harding rested a gentle hand on Haley's shoulder. "Do you want to go with him?"

She turned to meet his mother's warm brown eyes. They were so much like Asher's. "Are you sure you don't want to ride with him?" Haley asked.

Mama Harding pointed to Lucas's truck. "I'll ride with Lucas. I've never been a fan of seeing my boys in pain, and I can do my part from anywhere."

Haley wrapped her arms around Mama Harding's neck and squeezed. "Thank you." Haley released his mother as quickly as she'd grabbed her up. Turning to Asher, she brushed her hair out of her face. "Is it okay if I ride with you?"

"Of course," he said with a smile.

Haley smiled back. "Okay. I'll be right here."

She followed Noah into the ambulance once he'd

secured the gurney. Sitting beside Asher, she repeated, "I'm right here."

She meant those words now and forever. She intended to take her place beside the man she loved, and now was the perfect time to start.

CHAPTER 27
ASHER

No one in the ambulance said much on the drive to the hospital. Noah checked vitals and administered an IV in case of internal bleeding. Haley sat stoic beside him. Asher silently watched her. Sometimes, she lowered her chin and closed her eyes, and he knew she was praying. Then her gaze would travel up and down his body, assessing him for injuries.

He squeezed her hand from time to time, and she would smile. That was all he needed to push through the pain. He'd be lucky if he came out of this without a handful of broken bones, but he prayed for the best outcome. Anything that didn't involve surgery would be okay in his book.

When they arrived at the hospital, Asher closed his eyes as Noah and Jameson transported him inside. Being helpless and bumping on a gurney was not his idea of a good day, but with Haley beside him, it was tolerable.

Minutes later, the doctor approved him to be moved to the bed. She gave orders to the nurse for tests before slipping out.

The young nurse clicked rapidly at her computer. "How in the world did you end up like this?" she asked, focused on her reporting.

Asher grunted. "Fell off a tractor."

"Good grief. That sounds rough." The nurse continued to click away at the computer.

Asher didn't respond. He closed his eyes and took a few ragged breaths through his nose. This was the worst time to be immobilized. Haley was supposed to be on the road to spend Christmas with her family, not holed up in a hospital room with him.

He'd had high hopes for this day. He'd planned to tell Haley that he loved her, and he'd done that, but the circumstances hadn't been the best. His idea for the grand love confession had included a lot more hugs and kisses.

Asher huffed and twisted his mouth to one side. How was he going to get another one of those steal-your-breath kisses when he was laid up in bed? The thought made him smile, and the pain diminished for a moment. Barring surgical intervention, he wasn't going to let a few aches and pains stop him from kissing Haley before she left.

"I'll be back to get you in a little bit for x-rays. Let's give those pain meds time to kick in." The friendly nurse wrote her name on a white board before stepping out of the room.

When he was finally alone with Haley, he hid every reaction to the pain and turned to wink at her. Her slow smile sent a jolt of energy through his body, and the pain began to diminish.

Haley began humming as soon as the nurse was out of sight.

"Very funny," Asher said, narrowing his eyes.

Haley shifted from humming to singing the chorus of "Mamas Don't Let Your Babies Grow Up to be Cowboys."

"It's not always like this, you know," he said.

"I know, but you scared me today." Haley's playful expression fell.

Asher reached out his arm for her. "Thanks for coming to my rescue."

Haley chuckled and scooted her chair closer to his bed. "I would never hesitate to come running if you needed help, but please don't scare me like that again."

He linked her fingers with his. "I can't promise that, but I'll try my best." He brushed his thumb over the smooth skin on the back of her hand. "I'm sorry. I wanted to see you before you left, but I didn't plan to do it like this."

Haley's gaze skimmed over his face, and she

brushed her fingers over his forehead and through his hair. "I wouldn't leave without seeing you. I found this super sweet love note in my room this morning, and I couldn't leave without telling you that I love you too."

He brought her hand to his mouth and kissed it. "You need to get on the road. I'd rather you drive in the daylight."

Haley shook her head. "I'm not leaving."

Asher sighed, afraid he'd messed up her Christmas plans. "But you have to make it home for Christmas. There's a song about it and everything."

Haley brushed her fingers over his face and smiled. He could get used to her gentle touches. He was too focused on how good it felt to have her hands on him to even think about the pain.

"I'm staying. I texted Beth, and she said she would let everyone know what's going on."

He squeezed her hand. "But it's Christmas, Hales."

"And I'll be celebrating with the Hardings this year. I'm sure Mama won't mind adding a few more nights to my stay."

"If you go now and spend Christmas with your family, I might be well enough to travel soon, and I can come visit you."

Haley lifted her eyebrows and averted her gaze. "Actually, I was thinking I could stay here for

Christmas and we could visit my family for New Year's. If you're feeling up to it, of course."

Asher chuckled. "I can't argue with that plan."

Haley tilted her head and continued brushing her fingers through his hair. He was pretty sure the love of a good woman was the most powerful medicine he'd ever received. He couldn't think about anything except her green eyes. They had an aqua ring around them, making the irises a stark contrast to her fair skin.

"I love you," she whispered. "And I love the song." She brought her gaze to meet his, stealing his breath quicker than the jarring fall. "I need you to get to feeling better so you can play it for me." The fingers that had caressed his cheek slowly fell below his jaw and down his neck.

A knock at the door caused him to jerk, and he sucked in air through gritted teeth.

"Knock, knock," the young nurse mimicked as she walked into the room. "Ready for x-rays."

Asher was still trying to catch his breath after the stab of pain that had pulled him swiftly out of contentment. "Perfect timing."

Haley released his hand and stepped back. "I'll wait here until you get back. I'll call your mom and let her know how things are going."

"Thanks. Maybe call Micah. Mom doesn't answer her cell phone much, and I doubt she remembered to bring it." He grinned, still stunned by the powerful woman God had led into his life. "I'll see you soon."

As the nurse wheeled him away in the bed, Asher immediately felt the urge to be back with Haley. Every second felt too precious to squander, and he wanted her by his side for the rest of his days.

CHAPTER 28
HALEY

Asher was released a few hours later with two broken ribs. It was the absolute best they could've hoped for, and Haley had already said half a dozen prayers of thanks.

She followed the nurse who wheeled him out of the hospital to where Micah was waiting. Asher moved at a snail's pace as he stood from the wheelchair and tested the best way to hoist himself into Micah's truck.

Haley reached to help him, but Micah shook his head. She hadn't realized Asher might want to help himself, but it made sense. Her dad had always been fiercely independent, and she saw the good it could do in this situation. He wouldn't know his limits unless he tested himself.

Asher held tight to Haley's hand on the way back

to the ranch. Asher kept his eyes closed and his head leaned back.

They'd been driving for a few minutes when Asher grunted. "Can you turn on the radio?"

Micah punched the button. "What station?"

"You pick, Hales." He kept his eyes closed. His jaw tensed at every bump in the road.

"Um. Anything country."

Micah scanned through a few stations before settling on one playing a fast-paced song about how much he loved his pickup truck.

"Nope," Asher quipped.

Haley chuckled. "Anything a few decades older?"

"Oh," Micah said as he scanned a few more stations.

When a familiar Tim McGraw song filled the cab, Haley touched Micah's shoulder. "That's good."

She wasn't sure if Asher was asleep or just tolerating the ride, but no one spoke the rest of the way to the ranch. Haley didn't mind. Asher was beside her with minimal injuries, and she was headed to the place she loved—his home.

Her trip to Blackwater had gone much different than she could've expected. The man in the front seat wasn't the one she was meant to be with, but meeting him had led her to the right man for her.

Back at the ranch, Micah dropped Asher and Haley off at the main house at his request. Why hadn't he asked to be dropped off at his cabin? She hadn't seen Asher's place yet, and a surge of adrenaline lit her from the inside out. What would his cabin look like? Was he a slob?

Haley slid from the high truck and walked around the back to Asher's side. He was easing himself to the ground with a scrunched up nose.

"You okay?" she asked.

"Yep." Asher's voice was hoarse as he straightened and reached for her hand. He called over his shoulder to Micah, "Thanks for the lift."

Micah leaned out his window to say, "See you in the morning." He hadn't even gotten out of the truck.

Blues and whites blended in the sky. Slate-blue clouds dotted here and there, but the sun dominated the midday scene.

Asher leaned over as they ascended the first step to the porch. "I don't want to be away from you tonight. I'll just sleep here in one of the guest rooms."

Her heart did a happy dance knowing she would be near him for the rest of the day. She wanted to be accessible in case he needed help. Not that he would ask for it.

She ascended the stairs just behind him. He wasn't grunting as much as before, and she hoped the pain meds were working.

They chose the guest room closest to Haley's, and she helped him get settled in the bed.

"You haven't eaten anything today. What can I bring you?" Haley asked.

Asher closed his eyes and shook his head. "I'm fine for now. I think I'll take a nap while the pain meds are working." He lazily opened his eyes and his lips stretched into a slow grin. "You go get something to eat. You haven't had anything either."

"Okay. I'll check on you in a bit. Get some rest while you can."

"Thank you." He reached for her hand, and his eyes fell closed.

She kissed his forehead and slipped from the room. Relief washed over her as she leaned her back against the door. In many ways, she was thankful for Gabby's advice to wait and be patient. Haley had been absolutely sure of her feelings for Asher and the connection they shared before she rushed into a relationship. She and Asher were on the same page, and she wasn't worried about what the future might bring for them. They were equally committed to each other.

But she was also glad that everything was out in the open. Haley wore her emotions on her sleeve, and now she knew the urgency of sharing the joy of love. Things could have gone very differently today, and she was glad he knew that she would stand beside him through anything.

She pushed off the door and made her way

downstairs, hoping Mama Harding would have some leftovers she could snag.

Their relationship had started off in one of the "for worse" times mentioned in so many wedding vows, and it made her heart lighter to know that she and Asher could weather the tough times. Others might have given up, but she couldn't think of anything she'd rather do than be a helpmate to Asher.

Camille had served the frozen soup for lunch in Mama Harding's absence, and Haley stopped to chat with Camille in the meeting room while she ate. Camille shared the story of Noah's leg injury earlier in the year, and Haley got a little queasy just hearing about the bear attack. She wondered how often the men found themselves in dire situations. Instead of dwelling on the odds, she closed her eyes and said a prayer of thanks for the Lord's protection.

The door to Asher's room was still closed when Haley snuck back into her room. She left the door to her room ajar and pulled out her laptop to get some work done while Asher slept. A notification caught her eye, and she jumped for joy when she realized the bed and breakfast had its first online reservation.

Throwing her laptop onto the bed, she quickly slipped downstairs to celebrate with Camille. Mama Harding joined them, and the three women squealed and hugged in celebration. Haley returned to her work upstairs with a happy heart. The successes of the Hardings had become important to her, and warmth filled her chest as she realized this family loved her just as much as she loved them. Coming to Blackwater had changed her life. How many people were blessed with a wonderful family and then adopted into another? She tried to temper her excitement, but she'd never been good at squashing her feelings, especially happiness.

She peeked into Asher's room, but his eyes were still closed. The door creaked as she pulled it closed, and she heard Asher's whisper.

"Haley?"

"Yeah. It's me. I didn't mean to wake you."

He lifted his hand and beckoned her. She stepped to the bed and sat beside him. "How are you feeling?"

"Well, I tried to get up a few minutes ago, and that was a bust."

Haley chuckled. "Here. Let me help you."

She wrapped her arms around his back, splaying her hands on his broad shoulder blades and pulled him to sitting. By the time she'd helped him to his feet, his breathing was ragged, but he wrapped his arms around her, pulling her close.

"Are you okay?" she whispered.

Asher pulled back and nodded slowly. His gaze brushed over every inch of her face, and her heart raced as his attention slid to her mouth. His hands threaded into her hair, and his whisper sent a thrilling chill down her spine.

"I love you."

The powerful words hit her in the chest, and she raised her attention to his eyes. The look of adoration he gave her was enough to write an epic love story.

Their love story.

"I love you too."

It wasn't enough. Words would never be enough, but she made a vow to spend every day showing Asher how much he meant to her. She would be here while he recovered, and if he was feeling better, they could visit her family soon. She could think of a lifetime of firsts they could experience together.

His smile grew, sending her heart thundering again just before he dipped his head to seal his lips with hers.

His mouth slid leisurely against hers, sending sparks from her lips to her toes. One of his hands stayed threaded into her hair while the other slid down to wrap around her waist, pulling her impossibly close.

She'd never been kissed like this before. She'd never felt so cherished. Their first kiss had been eager and curious while this one was slow and adoring. Silent words flowed into her, and she felt his love in each movement. The rest of the world faded away as he wove their hearts and lives together. She was glued to him, and each move of his lips against hers felt like a whispered promise.

He pulled away gently and sucked in a deep breath before opening his eyes. "I intend to love you forever. Are you okay with that?"

Haley nodded. "I can handle that."

Asher took her hand in his and threaded their fingers together. "Good. I'm starving, and I smell food."

Haley chuckled. "It's suppertime."

Asher turned and shuffled into the hallway, holding onto the doorframe for balance. "Race you down the stairs."

She threw her head back and laughed. Asher rested a hand on his lower back and limped ahead of her.

Life with Asher Harding would never be boring.

CHAPTER 29
HALEY

"Are you sure you're up for this? I don't think this is medically advised," Haley said.

Asher only winced a little as he climbed into the passenger seat of her car. "Ladies, start your engines."

Haley raised her eyebrows at him as she started the car. "Last chance to back out."

Asher leaned back in his seat and turned to her. "I'm going to Fort Collins with you. I'm not backing out."

"Okay. Just checking." She turned to back out of the place she'd parked at the main house, and Asher laid a hand over hers.

"I'm sure about this, Hales. I want to meet your family."

"Well, you already met Beth, but she's not an indication about what to expect from the rest of the

Meadows. Neither am I. You basically already met the two crazies."

He squeezed her hand as she turned the wheel toward the drive leading out to the main road. "If you're crazy, then I'm crazy too."

Haley laughed high and loud.

"What?" Asher asked. "There's nothing wrong with being head over heels in love with a spontaneous red-head who nurtured me back to health."

She felt the heat creeping up her chest and into her face. She'd never met a man so open about his feelings before, and the rush of his affection was overwhelming.

She had seven hours with Asher all to herself, and they didn't waste a minute. They played twenty questions, name that song, and the ABC game the whole way to Fort Collins.

I t took most of the day to make the drive from Blackwater to Fort Collins. Asher and Haley stopped a handful of times to walk around, and they'd taken the scenic route through town to see her old school. Asher asked a million questions about her life growing up, and she wasn't sure what to think about his interest. No other man she'd dated had wanted to know anything about her, and Asher was eager to know as much as he could.

When they pulled up at her parents' house, she

parked and watched for Asher's reaction to the old home. It was large, as was necessary for the crew of Meadows siblings, but it wasn't boisterous or showy. Haley's family hadn't ever put much value in things, and that was something she'd loved about the Hardings. She would always put people and kindness over material things.

Asher didn't take his eyes off the house as he asked, "What are your aunts' names again?"

Haley leaned over and kissed his cheek. "Don't worry. They'll love you whether you remember their names or not."

He turned his attention to her. "Would you still love me if I forgot your name?"

She patted his shoulder. "Let's don't find out."

They got out of the car, and Asher stretched his arms above his head with a groan. "That happened to Noah."

Haley's ponytail slung over her shoulder as she whipped her head to him. "What?"

She opened the trunk and Asher reached in for their bags.

"Camille forgot him." He grunted as he pulled her suitcase out.

"No she didn't," Haley said.

"She definitely did. She lost a lot of her memory in a car accident."

Haley grabbed the last bag and closed the trunk.

"Mama Harding told me something about a car accident, but I didn't realize Camille lost her memories."

"So, my question still stands. Would you still love me if I forgot your name?"

Haley grinned and stroked his cheek. "You could forget my name, but you'd still be you, and I would still be me."

He leaned down and kissed her hard and quick. "You're right. And I definitely wouldn't forget you."

"You say that like Camille had a choice."

"She didn't, but I'm being romantic and whimsical. I know you like it."

Haley turned around to confront him, but he stifled her outrage with a wink.

"You're right. I like it when you talk pretty to me, but don't use it against me."

Asher shook his head. "I make no promises."

Haley narrowed her eyes at him and continued walking.

Asher whispered behind her, "Except to love you forever."

She couldn't contain her happiness. Asher was the perfect man for her. He was funny and sweet at all the right times, and he'd proven that he would stand beside her through the toughest times.

Now, she'd just have to hope he survived a weekend with her crazy family.

Haley's parents were waiting for them and ran

outside to help with the luggage. Her mom wrapped Asher in a hug, and he winced when she squeezed.

"It's so nice to meet you!" her mother cried. "Haley and Beth have both told me all about you."

"I've heard a lot about you too. Thank you for letting me visit this weekend. I wish we could have made it for Christmas."

Haley's mother stepped closer to her dad. "We understand. I'm so glad you're feeling better."

"Getting better every day. I'll be glad when this is all healed."

Haley's dad stuck out a hand to Asher. "I'm Bill, and this is Marianne."

Marianne covered her cheeks with her hands. "I'm sorry. I was so excited to meet you that I forgot to introduce myself." She wrapped Haley in a hug and swayed. "I missed you."

"I missed you too, Mom."

Marianne and Haley showed Asher to his room, then Marianne left them alone so he could get settled in.

"Are you sure it's not too weird to stay with my parents?" Haley asked.

"I'm fine here. Really. Your parents are great." He sat on the bed and patted the blanket beside him.

Haley smiled and took the seat beside him, cuddling to his side while trying not to touch his injury. "I'll be in the room across the hall tonight."

He pulled her in closer and kissed the top of her

head. "I'm excited to ring in the new year with you tonight."

"Me too. I think Jess and Beth are coming, but Gabby and the guys can't make it."

"That's a shame. I was hoping to meet everyone."

"We'll have plenty of time for that."

A door slammed downstairs, and Jess's youthful voice filled the house. "Haley!"

Haley jumped to her feet. "Jess is here!"

Asher stood slowly. "You go ahead. I'll be right behind you."

She chuckled and grabbed his hand. "I'll walk with you. I don't think you'll be running down stairs for a while."

He gave her hand a squeeze, and they worked their way to the stairs. Haley yelled, "Coming, Jess!"

Jess met them at the bottom and barreled into Haley for a hug. "I said yes!"

"Ah!" Haley squealed and hugged her sister tighter. "I'm so happy for you!"

She released Jess and pulled Asher closer. "This is Asher. The one I've been telling you about."

Jess raised her brows and offered Asher a hand. "Well, hello. I've heard wonderful things about you."

"Back at you." He turned to Owen who stood grinning behind Jess. "You must be the lucky man."

A slight blush colored Owen's cheeks. "That I

am. It's good to meet you. Jess hasn't stopped talking about you since Haley told us you were coming."

"I'm lucky I made it. She almost left me at a gas station."

Haley playfully pinched his arm. "I didn't leave you."

"Okay, well, she started moving before I had both feet in the car."

Jess laughed loud and high like a happy kid. "Hales, don't run him off."

Haley wrapped an arm around Asher's back and tilted her head up to him. It still felt like a dream that he was standing here beside her in her family home, but it was more like an answered prayer.

Asher kissed her forehead. "She's not getting rid of me that easily."

The rest of the night was just as perfect as Haley had always dreamed it would be. Seeing how easy things were with Asher, she understood why no other relationship had ever come close to working. He was the one for her—so perfectly imperfect just like her. He understood her humor, he didn't leave her side when she was scared, and he wasn't afraid to tell her exactly how he felt about her.

Later in the evening, Haley was in the kitchen when the countdown began, and she quickly shoved her empty dish into the sink and turned to run back into the living room. A chorus of "Ten, nine, eight" spurred her into action, but when the countdown hit six, Asher rounded the corner.

The fire in his eyes stole her breath and stopped her hurried steps. She'd been running for Asher, but he'd come for her first.

As her family marked the last seconds in the living room, Asher cupped Haley's face and kissed her through the end of the year and the beginning of the next. When he pulled away, she took a deep breath and sighed.

He leaned in again to whisper close to her ear, "Happy New Year, Hales."

She dug her fingertips into the back of his neck as his words sent a tingle down to her toes and drowned out the celebrations of her family in the next room.

"Happy New Year," she whispered back.

He nuzzled his face into her hair and pulled her closer. "I love you."

Those tiny words danced through the scars of her heart, filling them until it was made whole again.

CHAPTER 30
ASHER

Asher heard the clanging of cups and pans in the kitchen just after six in the morning. He eased out of bed as fast as his injuries would let him and threw on some decent clothes. He wanted to beat Haley to the kitchen, but he moved slowly without her help.

He slipped out of the guest room and tiptoed down the stairs. Haley's mom was pouring a cup of coffee, and her dad was reading a magazine at the bar.

Marianne heard him slip in and greeted him with a smile. "Good morning. How do you like your coffee?"

"Black will work just fine."

She handed him the cup she'd just poured and grabbed another for herself. "You're sure up early. There aren't any ranch tasks to tend to around here."

Asher brushed a hand through his tousled hair. "I know. I was hoping to catch you two before Haley got up."

"Morning!" Beth sang as she walked into the kitchen and straight to her dad, wrapping him in a tight hug.

"Beth, Asher wants to talk to us." Marianne's eyebrows rose, silently begging Beth to leave.

"It's okay," Asher said. "I don't mind if Beth is here. I just don't know when I'll see you again. I wanted to talk about Haley."

"Oh no," Marianne wailed. "Did she run you off? That poor girl comes on too strong."

"No, no," Asher said, raising his hands to stop Marianne from spiraling. "It's actually the opposite. I know we've only known each other for a month, but I know Haley is the one. I wanted to ask for your blessing to marry your daughter."

Marianne covered her mouth, and tears rolled down her cheeks shortly after.

Bill asked, "Which one?"

Asher fell into a fit of laughter and groaned, holding his side until the spasms stopped. "Haley. I want to marry Haley. Not today, but soon."

Marianne had her arms around him in an instant, and he tried not to grimace when the pain shot through his middle.

Beth crossed her arms over her chest with a smirk. "I knew it."

Asher gave her a wink. He liked that Beth looked after Haley. She needed someone in her corner who wouldn't chastise her for going after the things she wanted in life.

"I guess that's a yes for me too." Haley's father stood and removed his glasses before patting Asher on the shoulder. "Take care of her."

Asher nodded. "Of course, sir."

Bill narrowed his eyes and grinned beneath his mustache. "You can't even walk."

"I don't care," Asher said. He smiled at Bill's taunt. "I would do anything for her."

Marianne wiped her eyes. "I'm going to miss her."

Bill wrapped his arm around his wife. "We all will."

Beth threw her hands in the air. "In case you were waiting for my approval, I freely give it. You two are great together." She walked around the island in the center of the kitchen to Asher. "Haley's love is all-consuming, and you're probably the only one who isn't afraid of her. She just needed to find someone who would love as hard as she does."

Asher pulled Beth into a side hug. "You don't need to apologize for her, and you don't need to worry about me. If her biggest flaw is that her heart is too big, I'll count myself blessed."

Marianne pulled a skillet from a cabinet and

placed it on the stovetop. "We better get started on breakfast. Haley will be up soon."

"Good morning!" Haley bounced into the kitchen with energy to spare. "The coffee smells amazing."

She cuddled up to Asher's side and gave him a quick kiss. It wasn't nearly enough, but he'd take what he could get.

"Morning, sunshine. How did you sleep?" he asked.

"So good. Guess what? Mama Harding called me this morning, and they've filled all of the guest rooms for the next few weeks! She wanted to know if I could come back and help out."

Asher's eyes widened. "Really? Is that what you want to do?"

Haley nodded. The quick movement of her head had her ponytail bouncing. "She said she'd get Noah and Lucas to fix up a cabin for me." She bit her bottom lip before asking, "Is that okay with you?"

"Are you saying you're coming to stay for good?" Asher's heart raced in his chest as he dared to hope.

"Maybe. Probably. It depends on what you think of the idea."

He pulled her in and tolerated the pain in his ribs long enough to hold her. "I definitely want you to come home with me for good."

She bounced out of his arms with a squeal before shouting, "I'm moving!"

Marianne started crying again and dropped the spatula to hug Haley.

Bill quirked his mouth to one side. "I guess we'll be visiting the ranch soon."

Asher nodded. "We'd love to have you."

Haley grabbed Beth's hand. "I have to pack up some things at my apartment today. I'll come back for the rest later. Are you free today?"

Beth rolled her eyes. "I guess I am if you're moving out of state and need help packing."

Haley looked at him, and his heart beat faster. The woman he loved was coming home with him. If he had his way, they'd be married by the end of spring.

He pulled her to his side and whispered against her hair, "I love you."

She answered him with a kiss just like the one that had started it all.

EPILOGUE

MICAH

Micah swallowed hard and fought the urge to tug at his collar. He was thankful Haley hadn't made him wear a tux, but a suit and tie was almost as bad. There wasn't enough slack around his neck, and the material stretched tight across his broad shoulders.

He was in charge of transporting Asher and Haley's wedding gifts from the church. Everyone had just made it back to the ranch after the reception, and Micah parked behind another truck at the main house.

Asher greeted Micah as he killed the engine. "Thanks for this."

"No problem. The smaller ones are in the back seat." He resisted the urge to shiver against the cold March wind as it hit his neck.

Asher opened the door, and they took turns

moving the gifts from the truck to the meeting room. The last gift was much larger than the others. It was a flat square that barely fit in the bed of the truck.

"What do you want to do with that one?" Asher asked.

Micah shrugged. "Ask Haley if she wants to open it out here and tell us where to put it."

Asher jogged inside and Micah stepped closer to the large present. It was wrapped in cream-colored paper with gold designs. The tag on the front read "To Asher and Hales. From Noah and Camille." The embellished letters were definitely Camille's, and Micah groaned. Any gift from Camille would be over the top and no doubt impractical. It would also be something Haley would love. Camille had a knack for matching the gift to the person receiving it.

Micah folded his arms over his chest. Maybe that's why Camille had so many friends. She spent a lot of time getting to know people.

He twisted his mouth to the side, remembering his Christmas gift from Camille. She'd had his boots resoled—something he'd desperately needed but hadn't taken the time to do himself in the last six months.

Asher appeared a minute later dragging a smiling Haley behind him. She still wore the white dress she'd changed into for the reception, and her auburn hair was pulled up into a curly bun.

"What is it?" she asked, rubbing her hands together against the cold.

Micah raised his hands. "I have no idea. Just open it and let me know if you want me to drop it off at your cabin or somewhere else." He wondered if it would fit in Haley or Asher's tiny cabins. The new couple had plans to move Haley's stuff into Asher's place this week before leaving for their week-long honeymoon at a ski lodge in Freedom, Colorado.

Haley climbed into the back of Micah's truck with Asher's help. Her heels clanged against the metal of the truck bed as she stepped up to the present.

"It's from Camille!" Haley ripped into the wrapping paper and gasped. "It's a sign!"

Asher pulled his bride in close. "Wow. That's cool. It's the logo you made."

Micah studied the stainless steel piece as Haley ripped away the remaining paper covering. "Is it for the ranch?"

Haley brushed her fingers over the letters. "Yeah. I designed a logo for the website a few months ago, and she had it made into a sign. The one out by the road is rusted. I love it!"

Haley stepped back to reveal a large horizontal oval. A backwards B rested against an R in the center, and the words Blackwater Ranch lined the top just inside the oval perimeter.

Micah rubbed his chin. "It looks great." Haley certainly had a gift for design.

She turned to him and clasped her hands beneath her chin. "Can you put it up? Please."

Micah nodded. "Sure. Just leave it there and I'll take it to the road."

Haley squealed and wrapped her arms around his neck. He remembered the awkward conversation they'd had when Haley had showed up at their door four months ago. He was reminded how things had worked out for the best. Haley and Asher were just alike.

They stepped down from the bed of the truck, and Haley ran inside. Asher followed her, satisfied that his wife was happy on their wedding day.

Micah got back into the truck and started the engine. The exhaust from the truck billowed into the cold Wyoming air, obstructing his rear view in the side mirror.

He stopped at the nearest barn first to grab a ladder, and he contemplated changing clothes. The rust from the old sign would no doubt ruin his white shirt. No, he'd just be careful. He wanted to get the job over with and grab a bite to eat at the main house before sunset.

The driveway leading back to the main road was well worn today. Dozens of vehicles had driven over the snow, creating a muddy slush. He parked by the old sign at the entrance to the ranch and left his truck running. Climbing into the bed of the truck, he moved the bulky sign just enough to reach into the tool box behind it. He grabbed his biggest pliers and checked the back of the new sign to see what he'd need to hang it. Satisfied that Camille had done her homework, he jumped off the truck.

Twenty years ago, he'd helped his dad, Silas Harding, install the weather-worn sign. They'd built a wooden stand out of two large trunks and one that rested over the top of them. Micah propped the ladder against the pole on the right side first and climbed it to release the chain from the metal hook drilled into the hard wood. When he let it go, the sign hung limp from the remaining chain.

After repeating the task on the other side, he let the old sign fall to the snowy grass below before climbing down from the ladder. When his boots hit the frozen ground, he heard a vehicle coming. An older model sedan was puttering toward him. He turned his attention back to his work and trudged through the thick, dead grass to retrieve the new sign.

He'd barely made it to the tailgate of the truck when the constant hum of the engine driving by slowed and died. Micah looked around the truck. The car was stopped in the middle of the lane ten yards from the entrance to the ranch.

When no one stirred inside the quiet car, he left his task to see if his help was needed. The closest neighbors were a dozen miles away, and town was another eight past that.

The engine wasn't smoking, so that was a good sign. He stepped up to the driver's door and saw a woman inside. Her head was bowed over the steering wheel that she gripped in both hands.

When the woman didn't stir, Micah knocked lightly on the window.

The woman jerked her head up and faced him, tucking her arms in close to her chest and shrinking away from him. Her long hair fanned out around her with the hasty movement. Her eyes were wide in terror.

Micah lifted his hands. He wanted her to see he wasn't armed, and hopefully she would figure out that he wasn't dangerous either. "You need some help?"

She hesitated, eyes scanning him and their surroundings. That's when he noticed the dark-blue coloring on her right cheekbone. When she caught him looking, she turned her face away from him.

No wonder she was jumpy. Anger and pity swirled within him, creating a confusing emotion he'd never experienced before.

"Hey, are you okay?" Micah tried his best to speak softly, but he'd always had a gruff way about him. He was direct and deliberate, even in his speech, and it often came across as brash.

The woman shook her head. "I'm looking for Blackwater Ranch."

Micah eyed the empty stand waiting for the new sign. He turned back to the woman and looked her up and down, unsure what she could be looking for at his ranch. But if this woman needed his help, he'd put everything else aside to make it happen.

"Looks like you made it."

OTHER BOOKS BY MANDI BLAKE

Blackwater Ranch Series
Complete Contemporary Western Romance Series
Remembering the Cowboy
Charmed by the Cowboy
Mistaking the Cowboy
Protected by the Cowboy
Keeping the Cowboy
Redeeming the Cowboy

Blackwater Ranch Series Box Set 1-3
Blackwater Ranch Series Box Set 4-6
Blackwater Ranch Complete Series Box Set

Wolf Creek Ranch Series
Complete Contemporary Western Romance Series
Truth is a Whisper
Almost Everything

The Only Exception
Better Together
The Other Side
Forever After All

Love in Blackwater Series
Small Town Series
Love in the Storm
Love for a Lifetime

Unfailing Love Series
Complete Small-Town Christian Romance Series
A Thousand Words
Just as I Am
Never Say Goodbye
Living Hope
Beautiful Storm
All the Stars
What if I Loved You

Unfailing Love Series Box Set 1-3
Unfailing Love Series Box Set 4-6
Unfailing Love Complete Series Box Set

Heroes of Freedom Ridge Series
Multi-Author Christmas Series
Rescued by the Hero
Guarded by the Hero
Hope for the Hero

Christmas in Redemption Ridge Series

Multi-Author Christmas Series

Dreaming About Forever

Blushing Brides Series

Multi-Author Series

The Billionaire's Destined Bride

ABOUT THE AUTHOR

Mandi Blake was born and raised in Alabama where she lives with her husband and daughter, but her southern heart loves to travel. Reading has been her favorite hobby for as long as she can remember, but writing is her passion. She loves a good happily ever after in her sweet Christian romance books and loves to see her characters' relationships grow closer to God and each other.

ACKNOWLEDGMENTS

I needed a lot of advice while writing this book, and thankfully, I have some friends who spent a lot of time helping me. Thanks to my beta readers, Pam Humphrey, Tanya Smith, Jess Mastorakos, and Kendra Haneline. This story wouldn't have been as good without your help. I wouldn't know anything about horses without Melissa Taylor, so I owe her a big thanks for taking the time to teach me something new.

Thanks to my sister, Kenda Goforth, for being my cheerleader. Jenna Eleam, Stephanie Martin, Hannah Jo Abbott, and Elizabeth Maddrey, kept me focused when I thought this manuscript would fall apart. More thanks to my dad for teaching me about farm life, and thanks to my mom for being a dedicated reader.

Thank you to the many hands who helped create the book. Brandi Aquino with Editing Done Write made sure I used commas, and Amanda Walker gave this book its pretty cover.

And thank you for reading the book. I love writing, but it would be a lonely endeavor without the sweet readers who support me and encourage me to create these worlds and characters. You're the reason I get to keep writing and sharing what I love.

PROTECTED BY THE COWBOY

BLACKWATER RANCH BOOK 4

She's running from trouble, and now he's protecting more than just his ranch.

Laney Parker is in dire need of a fresh start. With broken bones and a broken heart, she shows up at Blackwater Ranch hoping to land the housekeeper position for the new bed and breakfast. When the caring family begins to ask questions, she struggles to trust them with her secret.

Micah Harding is the manager of Blackwater Ranch. His plate is full as it is, but something about the secretive stranger has captured his heart. Laney may be leading trouble to their door, but he can't help but think she's worth the risk.

Slowly, Micah shows Laney that she can trust him with her heart. When her past catches up to her, can his love save her in more ways than one?

Protected by the Cowboy is the fourth book in the Christian Blackwater Ranch series, but the books can be read in any order.

Made in the USA
Coppell, TX
24 July 2024